The Evil Men Do

An Ethel Thomas Detective Story

By Cortland FitzSimmons

Originally published in 1941

The Evil Men Do

© 2016 Resurrected Press
www.ResurrectedPress.com

Published by Resurrected Press

This classic book was handcrafted by Resurrected Press. Resurrected Press is dedicated to bringing high quality classic books back to the readers who enjoy them. These are not scanned versions of the originals, but, rather, quality checked and edited books meant to be enjoyed!

Please visit ResurrectedPress.com to view our entire catalogue, and like us on Facebook at Facebook.com/ResurrectedPress to stay updated!

ISBN 13: 978-1-943403-24-0

Printed in the United States of America

Resurrected Press Books in *The Chief Inspector Pointer Mystery* <u>Series</u>

RESURRECTED PRESS CLASSIC MYSTERY CATALOGUE

Journeys into Mystery
Travel and Mystery in a More Elegant Time

The Edwardian Detectives
Literary Sleuths of the Edwardian Era

Gems of Mystery
Lost Jewels from a More Elegant Age

Anne Austin
One Drop of Blood
The Black Pigeon
Murder at Bridge

E. C. Bentley
Trent's Last Case: The Woman in Black

Ernest Bramah
Max Carrados Resurrected:
The Detective Stories of Max Carrados

Agatha Christie
The Secret Adversary
The Mysterious Affair at Styles

Octavus Roy Cohen
Midnight

Freeman Wills Croft
The Ponson Case
The Pit Prop Syndicate

The Uttermost Farthing: A Savant's Vendetta

Arthur Griffiths
The Passenger From Calais
The Rome Express

Fergus Hume
The Mystery of a Hansom Cab
The Green Mummy
The Silent House
The Secret Passage

Edgar Jepson
The Loudwater Mystery

A. E. W. Mason
At the Villa Rose

A. A. Milne
The Red House Mystery

Baroness Emma Orczy
The Old Man in the Corner

Edgar Allan Poe
The Detective Stories of Edgar Allan Poe

Arthur J. Rees
The Hampstead Mystery
The Shrieking Pit
The Hand In The Dark
The Moon Rock
The Mystery of the Downs

Mary Roberts Rinehart
Sight Unseen and The Confession

Dorothy L. Sayers

Whose Body?

Sir William Magnay
The Hunt Ball Mystery

Mabel and Paul Thorne
The Sheridan Road Mystery

Louis Tracy
The Strange Case of Mortimer Fenley
The Albert Gate Mystery
The Bartlett Mystery
The Postmaster's Daughter
The House of Peril
The Sandling Case: What Would You Have Done?

Charles Edmonds Walk
The Paternoster Ruby

John R. Watson
The Mystery of the Downs
The Hampstead Mystery

Edgar Wallace
The Daffodil Mystery
The Crimson Circle

Carolyn Wells
Vicky Van
The Man Who Fell Through the Earth
In the Onyx Lobby
Raspberry Jam
The Clue
The Room with the Tassels
The Vanishing of Betty Varian
The Mystery Girl
The White Alley
The Curved Blades

Anybody but Anne
The Bride of a Moment
Faulkner's Folly
The Diamond Pin
The Gold Bag
The Mystery of the Sycamore
The Come Back

Raoul Whitfield
Death in a Bowl

And much more!
Visit ResurrectedPress.com
for our complete catalogue

LIKE us on Facebook for upcoming release
announcements!

Facebook.com/ResurrectedPress

FOREWORD

Cortland Fitzsimmons was best known for a series of mystery novels involving sports and other forms of popular culture. It was his novel *70,000 Witnesses: a Football Mystery,* that brought his talents to the attention of Hollywood when the novel was made into a film. This was followed several years later by *Death on the Diamond: A Baseball Mystery* which was also made into a movie. Other mysteries involved professional ice hockey, a dance band, and a stage magician. These mysteries were well written, fast paced, and entertaining, and one suspects, at least after the success of *70,000 Witnesses,* all were written with the potential for adapting them to film in mind.

As successful and popular as these mysteries were, Fitzsimmons' best work as a mystery writer may be four mysteries involving Ethel Thomas. It's hard to imagine a more unlikely detective. A seventy-five year old spinster at the time of the first mystery in which she figures, *The Whispering Window,* Thomas is a wealthy, unconventional member of New York's social elite. With the exception that she seems to know everything about everyone that matters, she bears almost no resemblance to that other famous female sleuth, Agatha Christie's Jane Marple. Whereas the latter confined most of her activities to a small English village, Thomas occupies a much larger village, the island of Manhattan. And rather than being prim and fussy, Thomas is not adverse to the occasional cocktail or whiskey and soda and fully enjoys an active social life with her many friends of a much younger age.

Considering that she was born about the time of the Civil War, Ethel Thomas has adapted remarkably well to the twentieth century. Telephones and radios no longer amaze her, she takes automobiles and airplanes in stride, and she has reveled in the changing fashions. A woman who was at her prime during the "Gilded Age" and the "Gay Nineties," she has made herself at home amidst the jazz and cocktail parties of the "Roaring Twenties" and the "Thirties." Shrewdness as a businesswoman has allowed her to weather the Depression with only minor concessions. And through it all she has kept her sense of humor and proclivity for making wry observations about the world around her.

The Evil Men Do finds Miss Thomas in a new setting, that of Hollywood, when she responds to a telegram from her niece Stella, an aspiring film actress, saying that she is in a "ghastly mess." The mess, of course, involves murder, but there is also blackmail in the wind, with all the activity centering around the mysterious Martinique, operator of an illicit casino on Sunset Boulevard. Miss Thomas has barely landed in California before she finds herself caught up in a murder investigation in which she is one of the prime suspects.

The motion picture business which serves as a background for the novel, was something that Fitzsimmons would have been familiar with as an insider, having been a successful screenwriter throughout the 1930's. His depiction of Hollywood is anything but glamorous, with several actresses willing to do anything as they compete for the same part, a dubious agent, an out of work extra making money on the side, and behind it all, Martinique, who seems to be able to call the shots because he has something on everyone.

It's rare for a man to have a female detective as a main character, but Fitzsimmons' portrayal of Thomas, a spry spinster younger than her years, whose acerbic comments enliven the novel is both lively and believable. Few male authors have created a female character as engaging and as entertaining as his Ethel Thomas. The problem is that she only appears in four books.

As with all of his works, *The Evil Men Do* is well paced and entertaining, a joy to read for anyone who likes their murders with a touch of humor. It should appeal especially to those readers who are fans of the movies of the 1930's, as with all of Fitzsimmons' works, it takes little imagination to envision the novel being made into a film

During the dozen or so years that marked his career, Cortland Fitzsimmons was both a successful author and screenwriter with over a dozen novels and as many movie scripts to his credit, including at least four film adaptations of his own novels. Today, though, he is unfortunately relatively unknown It is therefore with great pleasure that Resurrected Press offers this new edition of *The Evil Men Do*.

About the Cover

The cover of our edition of The Evil Men Do contain elements from the original cover of the first edition.

About the Author

Cortland Fitzsimmons was born in Brooklyn, New York (possibly Queens) on June 19, 1893 and died July 25, 1949 in Los Angeles, California. After attending New York University and The City College of New York, he worked for some time as a salesman for several book distributors and publishers before turning to writing full time in 1934. Most of his works as a writer were mysteries, a number of which were based on sports themes such as *70,000 Witnesses: A Football Mystery*, *Crimson Ice: A Hockey Mystery*, and *Death on a Diamond: A Baseball Mystery*. A number of his novels were made into films and he moved to Los Angeles to work as a screenwriter. His last book was a cookbook that he co-wrote with his wife Muriel Simpson *You Can Cook If You Can Read*.

Greg Fowlkes
Editor-In-Chief
Resurrected Press
www.ResurrectedPress.com
Facebook.com/ResurrectedPress

CHAPTER ONE

LOOKING BACK on the things that happened I suppose it was inevitable that Martinique should die. I had none of my premonitions about him, however, and must admit that his death, no matter how much I felt he deserved it, came as a shock and a surprise. So many things happened, so many people were involved in the preliminary stages leading to his demise that I was completely absorbed in them and blinded to the real flow of events. In review the steps are all clearly marked now and logical enough but then "hindsight" is always so annoyingly exact.

I knew absolutely nothing about the case that morning as the transcontinental plane circled over a valley hemmed in by mountains and I spotted the airport which meant Hollywood.

And there was no reason then for me to suspect the nervous girl with the wide, troubled eyes and tightly compressed lips as she too saw the field and turned from the window and slipped her arms into the sleeves of a mink jacket. I had been reading bulletins sent out by the Chamber of Commerce and sniffed at the idea of furs in sunny California.

She was impatient to land. A small sandaled foot tapped nervously on the floor beneath us. I wanted to tell her to stop lest she press a hole in the seemingly thin body of the plane and drop us into space to be spattered on the land rushing up so rapidly. I had been wondering about her, through the night, across the unreal desolation of the dust bowl slipping ghostlike beneath us, wondering why she nibbled at her nails until they were bleeding irregular scars. She was a blonde—not the hard brittle type, coldly antiseptic with fishy-blue calculating eyes. She was soft and cuddly, something to be held and treasured. A doll to be loved and cared for, a creature to be reassured. She needed someone then to smooth the wrinkles from her troubled brow, to banish the fear that haunted her lovely gentle eyes.

Was she, too, facing an unknown problem waiting for her just beyond that low ridge of mountains against which Hollywood snuggled or was she fully aware of her problem and ready to face it, fearful though she was, and devil take the consequences? Poor child! I wanted to help her, tried to engage her in conversation during the night but she had had no inclination to talk. She threw an armor of silence around her as she bit, bit, bit at her nails until I had wanted to slap her hands and say, "Don't! Only fools and idiots bite their nails. Which one are you?"

The other woman was just as eager to land. She had been the talkative type, telling me about Hollywood, her career, her ambitions. Fresh from a Broadway success she was answering a call from Hollywood to make a test for the part of Annabella in *The Tides*. "I made them come to me," she had said, sure of herself, poised yet eager, with sultry fires smoldering in her hazel eyes. Desire for the part was there too, and as I watched her, listened to her talk, I knew she'd move heaven and earth to get the cherished part.

"Seems silly to test me, Auriel Dodd, for a part, don't you think?" I knew nothing about it and was willing to agree with her but like a true Thespian she was sure of herself and rattled on: "Everyone knows what I can do, but there you are."

The plane made a long sweeping curve over the field to head into the wind, I suppose, or whatever it is they need to do. I always feel a little uneasy as a plane begins to land, the earth rushes up with such terrific speed as if it would clutch you and drag you down. I turned away from the window and for probably the twentieth time

read the frantic telegram which had made me—Ethel
Thomas, old lady, amateur detective and, I've heard it
said, busybody—make up my mind, and head for
Hollywood. The wire was from my grandniece, Stella
Wayne.

"Am in ghastly mess, trapped, no place to turn," I
read. "Can't tell Mother. Need you and your wits as they
have never been needed before. I'm desperate, I'm lost if
you don't come. Perhaps lost in spite of you." The minx!
That was in the nature of a challenge and she knew it.
"Please, Ethel, please help me! Come at once! Fly! Only
hurry! Hurry! Hurry!"

What woman could resist such an appeal, one filled
with such interesting possibilities even though they were
probably greatly and extravagantly exaggerated?

How typically Wayne in its disregard for money and
expense that telegram was! How like Stella when the
check-rein was off! How like all the Waynes, who never
did anything simply and calmly since the day over a
hundred years ago when young Silas Wayne married an
actress and faced his indignant family with her, forcing
them to accept her, to make her one of them despite their
horror that such a thing could happen to a Wayne. I had
known old Stella Wayne, the actress. She was an old
woman when I was a girl but it was she who had brought
fire and life into the stodgy blood of the smug Waynes—a
heritage that flared in the present generation. And
because of that woman I was floating over the Western
Airport, knowing nothing, fearing the worst, hoping for
the best. Stella was in some trouble, there could be no
doubt of that.

I had searched the papers for an inkling as to what
her trouble might be but there had been nothing unusual
about the Hollywood gossip. A brawl in a café wherein a
he-man, so-called, had tried to defend the integrity of his
manhood or something equally silly. A sordid story of a
divorce sensation. A suggested rumor of a new
breathtaking romance. The inevitable pictures of players;

but never a word of this catastrophe which had overtaken Stella. What public reputation I have has come to me because of my connection with several murder cases. I hope I am and have been a good friend in any emergency. I want to be. Would Stella send for me so frantically for anything short of murder? I had remonstrated against the thought of murder as I stepped into the plane at Newark and all the way across the country I kept saying like an old woman counting her rosary, "It must not be murder! Not for Stella!" I hoped that, at the worst, Stella had become involved with some unscrupulous scoundrel who could with proper technique be put in his place. But could it be that Stella had become entangled in a murder?

Murder! Surely not Stella! And yet why not? Human passions have no regard for money or family background. Even so-called nice people are only slightly veneered with a patina of civilization that can bear but little scratching. We are all elemental under the surface and have thoughts and desires that we keep locked deep within the recesses of our minds.

It could have been no simple situation that had prompted that telegram. Waynes are too prone to laugh at trouble. No! She would not have sent it so forcefully, would not have made it so irresistible unless . . . Could it be that she was in league with the agents who had been pestering me to take a writing job in Hollywood? Had she sold out to them just to get me on the ground? I have heard that they will stop at nothing to gain their ends. No! Not Stella. There was nothing underhanded about her. She would stoop to no such trick, not for the best agent in Hollywood.

"Can't tell Mother." That phrase stayed in my mind. Of course she couldn't tell Henrietta. No one had ever been able to tell Henrietta Wayne, née Osgood, anything except Emily Post whose rules for social living were Henrietta's Bible. And yet there had been times when Henrietta had disagreed with the always correct Emily, but that was when it was something that Henrietta wanted to do. She had her own rules, hard and fast, for her personal desires but they were always right, oh, horribly so. She would much rather be right than human. She was completely hemmed in by her social reservations and lived under an obsolete banner bearing the words, "It's not done." How a woman with freezing fluid in her veins had ever produced such glorious children I had never understood. She had been a dutiful wife, I had no doubt of that, and she must have given more to the reproduction of her kind than her cold dignified duty. If she did let down those cold barriers it remained a secret between her and her husband; the world never knew it. Tell Henrietta! I should say not, for she was as cold and beautiful as a pale green glacier and just as hard and unyielding. Imagine, if you can, confiding your troubles to a chaste electric refrigerator.

Poor Stella! She evidently needed an understanding confidante. My heart has ached for that sweet, impulsive, warmhearted girl, who as a child was of the earth, earthy and tried with a child's persistent lack of understanding to pierce the solid armor of her mother's composed, frigid reserve. I've seen her hurt, rebuffed and bewildered, covering her pain with a gallant smile which was a lie for the world to see.

What on earth had she done? Was this plea for help in some way connected with her career? I could still remember that scene in the Wayne living-room when Stella, marching in at tea time, her head up, shoulders squared, a new resolve in her gentian-blue eyes, as icily determined as Henrietta had ever been. I could see her and hear her saying in open revolt with all the Wayne devil-may-care courage, "Mother, I'm going to a theatrical school. I'm going to be an actress like Great-grandmother Wayne. I want nothing else."

The old ghost, quiet for many years, had reared its head in the Wayne's correct living-room and Stella standing there was very like that other woman who had stormed and subdued the citadel of Wayne stodginess.

Stella had raced on: "Don't argue and frown and don't try to get your own way by appealing to Father or crying and having a spell and don't try to talk me out of it. I've made up my mind. I'm partly your daughter, I've your dogged determination, but I'm also a Wayne and I have reached a point where I don't care. I've made up my mind. Further discussion will be useless."

It was. I could have cheered that valiant young girl who knew what she wanted and was determined to get it. Henrietta had nurtured a will stronger than her own. A will that knew how to battle her on her own ground with her own weapons.

That was three years ago. She had gone to school and then had given that up to do summer stock. From a summer theatre she had moved up to small parts on Broadway, had worked and struggled toward the top, doing it as a Wayne would, the hard way. Picture scouts had discovered her. And now because of all that I was nearing Hollywood.

From now on, no matter what comes or goes, I'll never again say, "I won't do this or that." All my life I have found myself forced into doing things I had thought never to do again, but that is because we can't control the flow of events, the flood of life that carries us with it. At last I know I'm a fool to fight something over which I have no control. I had said over and over that I would not go to Hollywood, but how futile my statements, because there I sat for all the world like an old fire horse waiting for the plane to land. I was really thrilled to be there.

I didn't, however, want to find Stella connected with a murder case. I didn't want her caught up in the meshes of a scandal which might affect the career which was her life. She had chosen motion pictures instead of the stage. I had opposed Hollywood, had wanted her to stay in theatre, believing that she could become the first lady of the stage, but she would not listen to my advice. She was picture-minded but she did promise to go on studying and working and she had declared, with some conviction, that she would not let Hollywood get her. Had it?

And how would this fabled place affect me? I had definitely made up my mind I would not go to Hollywood because for a month Hollywood had been calling me and I had turned a deaf ear to its golden, siren voice. I had been flattered and thrilled by the prospect, however, had even been tempted to take their fabulous offer just for the ride out there. It all happened after the publication of my second novel and its subsequent sale to one of the studios. I can understand the purchase of the book because it will, if it is not butchered too much, make a fairly decent picture. But why they should want me out there as a writer I can't imagine. The agent says my social register background has had something to do with that. I've heard of all sorts of reasons for going to Hollywood but the fact that your name is in the Blue Book is a new one and seems irrelevant.

They offered me a contract to prepare my story for the screen. I know I could do a good job at that because my people are human and I would keep them so instead of having them just sticks who move and are pulled about by attempts at being clever. I didn't want to go out there and write for the screen. Why should I? I have all the money I want and from what I have heard about the place it is just once removed from a madhouse. I said, "Nonsense!" to the elegant young man who called on me from an agency. Although he gave me the impression that I had committed a heresy I could not dampen his ardor. Perhaps it was his determination to earn a nice commission with the minimum of work that made him persist. Later that afternoon the same elegant young man with a voice that would melt a rock called me on the telephone to say that the studio had increased its offer by the sum of two hundred and fifty dollars a week. I said, "No!" quite emphatically and rang off. He called me again within three hours to inform me that he had boosted the offer another two hundred and fifty. Again, I said, "No."

My refusal of a proposition has never been worth so much before and I'm quite sure will never be so valuable again. Each time I refused them they raised the ante until I was afraid to answer the telephone or read a telegram lest I weaken. Among other things, I think, I am a business woman, and I must admit that it took a great deal of courage to keep turning down that salary. Just before I had definitely decided to leave town with no forwarding address I received Stella's wire. The urgency of the wire put a new aspect on the case. For Stella's sake it might seem better if I were ostensibly going to Hollywood to write than to be of assistance to her. I finally capitulated and agreed to work at a studio. I told them I would arrive in Hollywood in about one week from the day of the acceptance of the contract. I left New York at once.

My mind was not at rest on the trip out. When I wasn't thinking and worrying about Stella I was wondering how I could hope to fit into the scheme of operation of the motion picture industry—an old woman with thoughts and opinions of her own. A woman who had never done one day's actual work in a long lifetime. If only half the things I have heard about the picture business are true I would last about ten minutes. Yet I must admit I was torn by curiosity. I wanted to try it. I had to help Stella first, however.

Our pilot had set the plane down with hands as careful and tender as a lover's. We raced along the ground. There I was, arriving not as a writer but a woman with an S.O.S. clutched in her hand and wondering what it was all about. I was in no frame of mind for the beginning of a literary career but then the studio didn't expect me for a week and there was no need for them to know about Stella.

We taxied to a stop beside the exit gate with the nice precision of a settling gull. We were all anxious to land. The nervous blonde and Auriel Dodd seemed eager to be the first to alight. The little blonde looked out of the window. I saw a change come over her face. Was it fear? I could not tell. She sank back into a seat to open her handbag for an application of makeup. Auriel Dodd was quite ready to take first place—her makeup was perfect as she waited for her entrance cue to Hollywood.

Outside the plane the warm valley air caressed me. I was a moment finding my land legs as I stepped to the ground. It was a gay, busy place. Crowds of people gaped over the wire fence, down from the balconies and even from the tower top of the squat tile-covered building. Children with autograph books and ready pencils eyed us appraisingly and then with disgust for our anonymity on their urchin faces scurried away. They were looking for stars and we were but ordinary people of the planet earth. Auriel Dodd was unknown to them.

Men with briefcases under their arms dived for the exit to meet women whose warm, close embraces showed the anxiety they had lived through during the duration of the flight. I saw happy smiles, half-concealed tears of gladness, as I searched that line of faces for Stella or someone I knew. Surely she would send someone after receiving my wire. I felt a stranger in a strange land as I looked over that long line of faces.

A swarthy man had met Auriel Dodd and had her posing for pictures before cameramen. Flashlights popped. The autograph seekers ran back. In a moment Auriel Dodd was surrounded. She laughed, chatted, was graciousness itself as she enjoyed every minute. I heard her ask her companion, "Why didn't he come, Enrico?" His reply was muffled. She shrugged, and moved away down a lane of gaping admiring eyes.

As I watched them go the nervous little blonde came out of the plane and stood behind me for a moment, her harried eyes darting over the dwindling sea of faces. I turned and thought I saw her shudder but I was not sure. She was hesitant, troubled. I did wonder why when she had been so eager to alight she had suddenly changed her mind and, under the pretense of fresh makeup, had lingered in the plane until the Dodd procession had

trickled away. With mink coat hanging open she moved
forward with quick short steps. She looked neither to the
right nor the left as she went down the red carpet and
through the gate. I tried to make my smile friendly and
reassuring as she clicked by, but her curt nod was the
acme of indifference. I thought her eyes did light up in
swift recognition a second later and I turned to follow her
gaze, but there was no answering glow for her on any of
the blasé faces turned in our direction and her own eyes
had dimmed again. The girl worried me.

The last of the passengers had gone. I was alone a few
feet from the plane. Even the hostess, her responsibilities
over, had left. A porter, a smile on his dark, wide face,
ambled forward to take my bags. The gapers had left the
fence. The porter and I were alone in a strange world as
the plane swung and taxied toward the hangars. I felt a
little homesick and more than a little annoyed because in
all that crowd there was no known face waiting for me—
not even the Wayne chauffeur. I didn't expect Henrietta.
She was probably far too busy doing the proper social
thing with some set idea in her mind that it would benefit
Stella's career. Oh yes, Henrietta was in Southern
California. The one thing Stella had been unable to
accomplish was the complete divorcement of her life from
her mother's ever-watchful eye. Henrietta had moved to
the Coast and was no doubt making other Hollywood
mothers look pale and insignificant.

The porter lifted my luggage and waited, shifting his
weight from one foot to the other until I said, "I'll take a
cab."

In a few days I'd have my own staff, for Malcolm, my
chauffeur, was driving across country with Agnes, my
maid, and Debbie, my cook. They were having a vacation
of sorts and a trip which I had discovered was a wish
fulfillment, for Hollywood to them was what the Holy
Land must have been to a Crusader. No Moslem ever
turned his eyes toward Mecca with more ardor and zeal
than they contemplated Hollywood. Even staid and stolid

Malcolm was thrilled by the prospect of being able to gape at moving-picture stars. They were so excited, so delighted, when I suggested the trip that they brought out great quantities of moving-picture magazines from belowstairs just to prove to me how interested and glad they were to undertake the journey.

"You can go into town in the Company's car if it ain't gone. It's cheaper," the porter suggested.

Before I could reply I saw a young man coming through the doorway from the waiting-room and I knew instinctively that he was coming for me. As the porter waited for my answer the young man came forward quickly, a slim, hatless, sun-tanned giant with dark wavy hair, blue-black eyes that should have been full of laughter and weren't. He wore cream-colored slacks that slapped about his long straight legs, a rich-brown tweed sport coat and a polo shirt open at the neck. He essayed a troubled, rather grim smile as he said, "You are Ethel Thomas, Stella Wayne's aunt, aren't you?"

"Since you are looking for an old lady and I'm the only one left, your powers of deduction are not too remarkable," I replied. Then duplicating his bluntness I asked, "Who are you?"

"Peter Bradley. You are Stella's aunt, aren't you?"

"Did Stella send you for me?"

Some of the grimness left his face. "Yes, she did. She said I'd know you, could pick you out of a hundred old ladies, that you were one in a million. You are, you know." His smile was charming as he threw me that bit of flattery.

I'm helpless against such gracious charm, particularly from young men if they happen to be obviously troubled and spontaneous at the same time. I liked the boy. I smiled. "Where is Stella?" I asked.

"Working." His face sobered quickly. "I'm sorry I was late. I try to cut things too fine. I'll explain as much as I can as we drive in. If you'll wait here, I'll bring the car up to the entrance." He swung away in long easy strides but

I didn't wait. I followed him, the porter shuffling along beside me, to a gorgeous pale cream roadster. I sank into soft coffee-brown leather upholstery while the luggage was stowed in the rear. As we swirled away from the porter I said, "Well!"

"I'm not supposed to tell you a thing, Miss Thomas," he said as we raced down the long drive at a speed that warned me of the ride to come. We went through the entrance, the car rocking on its tires and groaning from the abuse. As the wheels straightened and the car bit into the road he went on, "Stella told me to ask you if you would mind using an assumed name for a few days."

"Whatever for?"

"An idea of hers."

"But doesn't she know I'm to be out here as a writer?"

A shadow fell across his face and there was disappointment in his voice. "Then you didn't come because she—"

"Of course I did and for no other reason. I don't report to the studio for a week and no one knows I am here nor do they expect me yet." I was annoyed and snapped that information at him. The next moment I regretted my annoyance and explained. "Since I was coming I thought I might just as well get some of the ridiculous money they offered me. Two birds with one stone, you know."

He laughed suddenly but its very explosiveness showed how nervous he was. "When do they expect you?" he asked, cutting his laughter short so that it still seemed to float in the air around us.

"In about a week. I didn't say when I'd arrive."

"They'll find out. They always do. They know everything. Hollywood's an odd place, Miss Thomas. It's news. There are gossip mongers with their stooges everywhere picking up crumbs of information. The whole town is . . . well, it's more than just a state of mind. It . . . I'm sorry you're going to work here."

That statement seemed a challenge. "Why?" I demanded.

"Because people do queer things out here. It may be the climate or . . . It may be ambition. I don't know. All I know is what I see. I don't know why."

What on earth was he driving at? I sat back and waited. I did not want to confuse his already troubled thought processes. They seemed muddled enough as it was. I hoped he was not going to be one of those people who never finished a sentence. Danglers, I call them. I was thinking of the shattered conversations I had endured during a long life when he went on.

"I'm in this thing too. If you help her, you'll have to help me, or . . . What I'm trying to say and doing so badly it that she wants you to help me because that will help her, She's . . . She's all mixed up, doesn't know what to do, where to turn, except to you. . . . And she's set her heart on the part. I think she'll die if she doesn't get it."

"Rubbish!" I snorted and then looked at his harried profile. He gazed straight ahead at the road, his nostrils tensed, his eyes pin-points of concentration. "How about your state of mind?" I demanded. "Don't you know that people don't die, even for love?"

He smiled, just a flicker that traced across his lips and vanished. "I want what she wants. I'd like to get it over with. You see I have no family to worry about, no part I want to play. There's no one who cares where I go or what happens to me . . . except Stella, and she . . ."

"She cares?" I asked.

"Oh, yes!" he answered quickly and his face glowed with the thought of Stella. It was a light turned on suddenly in the darkness. "She does, next to her career. We're in love, that's the hell of it. That's why she won't let me shoulder the thing alone, why she won't lie low and shift the responsibility. She's an adorable fool. She has so much to lose—position, career, family. They are all important to her, yet . . ."

"She is willing to throw them all away because of you and you are worried, afraid that you are not worth such a sacrifice. Is that it?"

"Yes. How did you know?" he asked surprised.

"Because you wouldn't be worth your salt if you didn't feel that way, because if you were less a man I doubt Stella would be in love with you, that's why. You see, I know Stella."

"Isn't she wonderful!" He actually beamed. "But she shouldn't do it, Miss Thomas. I don't want the specter of a lost career between us. It's different with a man. Things don't stick to a man the way they do to a woman, you know that."

"Of course I know it. What woman doesn't? A man can transgress most of the laws set down by society and we find some excuse for him but when a woman steps over the line, even in this day and age of sex freedom she is outside the pale."

"That's what I keep telling her," he insisted. "Perhaps you can reason with her. There are so many factors. You know her mother. How she . . . I don't mean to say anything against Mrs. Wayne but there she is and Stella . . . Well, naturally she doesn't want to hurt her mother's pride, but . . ."

"Peter, Peter, Peter!" I exclaimed. "For heaven's sake, stop breaking all of your sentences into bits. I'm dying of curiosity and you sit there and talk like a dangle-minded oaf."

He laughed. "I'm a little afraid of you."

"Of me!"

"Yes, you! I want you to like me. I want you on our side, but more than that I want your approval. I'm not a social catch, not good enough for Mrs. Wayne. I do have money but very little else in the way of background to offer. My people have always been cursed with respectability and very little else. My father made a great deal of money in oil and when he tried to play and have some fun both he and my mother were killed in an accident."

"What you are is the only thing that counts," I said.

"Not with a woman like Mrs. Wayne."

"We won't worry about her. Tell me more about yourself."

He was silent a few moments, devoting his attention to the road and his thoughts. "Perhaps I'm a fool," he said, breaking the silence, "but I don't believe real love is or should be possessive. You can't try to own a person, tell them what to do, or how to live their lives. You can't use your love as a means to an end. If you do, it becomes a club and is apt to kill the thing you love. I'm so mixed up. Do you mind my raving like this? I haven't known you ten minutes and yet I'm spilling over like a sloppy mill-pond."

"Talk away. I'm listening. You are confused. Better talk it out. Get your fear out into the open where you can see it, it's less formidable that way. Why are you afraid?"

"Stella is . . . No. I promised her I wouldn't tell you, but I can say this, Miss Thomas, and I know it will sound silly and melodramatic but I'm awfully afraid that Stella may do something that she will regret all the rest of her life."

"Don't you mean that you may regret it?" I asked.

He turned so suddenly, was so surprised, that we nearly ran off the road.

"What made you say that?" he asked.

"You. How will Stella's actions affect you?"

"I'm not modern enough to disregard a woman's virtue," he said.

"When it affects you," I added.

"I guess that's right," he admitted.

"You are making it sound like an old ten-twenty-thirty melodrama. Who is the villain in the piece?" I was a little disappointed. Had I been dragged across the country to advise a girl as to whether or not she should become a lady of uneasy virtue? No! Stella was not that type. If she wanted to give herself to a man she would do it and there would be nothing said about it one way or the other. There had to be something else and I was anxious to find out what it was. "When will I see Stella?" I asked.

"She'll come to the hotel as soon as she can."

My eyes had been busy as I listened. We had crossed a low sandy stretch of wasteland and were climbing toward higher ground. Ahead of us and to our right the Santa Monica mountains were taking definite shape, looming out of the haze which had blurred them from the airport.

"Stella thought you'd better go to a hotel. She didn't want her mother to know you were here until . . ."

Another sentence trailed off into space as he stopped talking and for a good reason. He was watching boulevard traffic as we came to a full stop and then joined the flow of swiftly moving cars.

"Until what?" I prompted as we joined and flowed with the racing cataract of cars.

"The blow strikes, I guess," he added with sudden despair.

"And is there no way to stop it?"

"That's what worries me. There is a possible way and I'm afraid Stella has made up her mind to take it. I can't let her do it, Miss Thomas, not if I have to kill another man to prevent it." He said it as simply as one says, "I must stop in at Woolworth's and get some of those cheap envelopes."

Merciful heavens! What a contradiction he was. He had just said that he thought possession killed love and yet he made such a statement. I studied him carefully. He was clean and fine and somehow made me think of the outdoors. I felt he should be on a horse rather than slumped in that sleek demon of the road. With his determined eyes on the traffic and that grim set to his jaw he had threatened to kill a man without the flicker of an eyelid.

So they were waiting for the blow to strike them, were they? As he threaded our way like a weaver-bug playing with the white lines of the highway, he seemed to have no idea that he had just delivered a terrific blow that left me limp and breathless with its possibilities. "Kill another man!" burned deep into my mind as we skimmed past a motion-picture studio and a sign which suggested, "Eat with the stars."

What man? Why?

We reached another intersection and turned into a broader highway bearing the legend, Cahuenga Boulevard. The mountains were close upon us now on both sides, bearing down, hemming me in with that thought, "Kill another man!"

In the bright, glorious California sunshine it was difficult to realize that once again I had been catapulted into grim, horrible melodrama, that at that very moment we were racing toward a tragic entanglement that would affect how many lives, that a man lay dead somewhere obviously undiscovered, that discovery must be imminent because Stella was ready to act, that the blow would strike and doubtless crush this grave young man, blast Stella's life and career and, I admit, I thought with a smile, give Henrietta an unforgettable case of jitters. The effect on Henrietta would be like the breaking up of an Alaskan ice jam.

He caught the flicker of that smile. "It's no laughing matter. I mean it." The words floated to me from the corner of his mouth.

"I don't doubt you for a moment. As a matter of fact, your driving is murderous," I snapped. "I'm not at all sure that either of us will live to help Stella or anything else."

"It's the way people drive out here. Everybody's in a hurry."

"Well, I'm in no hurry to die. Slow down!" He wove across traffic lines and settled behind a truck dribbling decomposed granite from its load. "I didn't mean to frighten you," he said.

"Suppose you tell me about this murder," I suggested.

"I promised Stella I'd wait. She'll be at the hotel. We'll tell you together. You'd better get it all in one dose anyhow. We're not quite agreed on the story, and . . . I'd better watch traffic. It gets thicker from here on." Without further comment, he devoted himself to the road.

I tried to relax against the swift mad flight of weaving, cross-cutting cars. "Suppose you tell me about the points of interest," I suggested with a gaiety I did not feel. "It's been many years since my last trip to California."

He agreed and spoke with the brevity of a train dispatcher. Names followed in rapid succession, names I had heard and read in the papers. Cahuenga Pass. The Cross on the Hill where the Passion Play was given. Hollywood Bowl. Symphonies under the stars. Highland Avenue. Hollywood Boulevard. The Hollywood Hotel. Grauman's Chinese Theatre. The Footprints of the Stars. La Brea. Sunset Boulevard, a thread of road running from the city to the sea. The Strip. Martinique's.

"Remember that place," he cautioned and his voice was hot and tense as we flashed by.

I caught a fleeting glimpse of a very smart building, its windows filled with adorable antiques. Over the windows there was a long sign and the legend: La Galerie Martinique.

Other attractive shops flashed by and soon we were in comparatively open country. On our short wild ride we had gone through a dozen community centers which reminded me of what that modern wit, Alexander Woollcott, had said about Los Angeles. It was something about twelve towns in search of a city.

Beverly Hills. It was a charming tree-filled town with gracious houses and beautiful gardens—a delightful residential city with flowers in profusion everywhere. I liked it at once.

In another moment we were at the hotel. It was soberly quiet and not at all what I had expected. If I had thought about it at all, I must have expected something sensational, garish and in bad taste. It was nothing of the sort; just quietly elegant, that was all.

The desk clerk was as solemn as a church-warden as he waited for the woman ahead of us to register. We stood next in line, Peter's firm young hand on my arm. The clerk produced a key, struck a bell and said, "Front! Miss French to three-fourteen!'"

Peter's fingers bit into my arm viciously so that I flinched with sudden pain. The woman turned round, giving me a surprised smile of recognition. It was my tortured nail-biting friend from the plane. So her name was French!

She turned. Her, "Hello, Pete," was a surprise.

"Hello, Alice," Peter replied.

She moved away behind the bellboy. Strange girl!

The church-warden clerk behind the desk waited with bored dignity to serve us. He was an elegant young man, much too good for the position he held. I was sure of that the moment I looked at him and later I was to learn that he was an infinitely better actor than some of the top-ranking stars but he had just never had the breaks.

Peter had stepped ahead of me and said, "The suite reserved for Miss Ethel Stevens. S-t-e-v-e-n-s." He spelled it out deliberately for my benefit. Poor lad! He was very obvious about it. Why on earth hadn't he told me about my assumed name? Since he didn't, I could have caught on without his being so obvious about it, but then he had no way of knowing that I can take a hint without being kicked into the next county.

I felt like an immoral woman as the clerk eyed us with mild, amused speculation behind those limpid gray eyes of his. If he thought Peter was my gigolo, I could stand it if Peter didn't mind. I registered with my usual scrawl and either in spite of my self-boasting about my perspicacity or because of pure unthinking habit I wrote Ethel Thomas across the line and then when I remembered, had to squeeze the Stevens into a space much too small for it.

"Cards ought to be larger," I suggested to the clerk as he meticulously printed my name over the signature. I was thinking how tactless that was when he looked up, gave me a wan smile, as if he had just read my mind and said prissily, "It's for the mail and telephone departments. Prevents mistakes."

As we followed the bellhop toward the elevators Peter asked, "Have you known Alice French very long?"

"Plane companion, nervous and upset, obviously in trouble. Know what it is?"

"No."

"Who is this French girl?"

"She is part of the story," he said gloomily, looking after her.

"What! And I flew across the country with her. If I had known . . ." I didn't finish, for Stella, lovelier than I remembered her, rushed across the lobby toward us.

"Oh, Ethel darling!" I was caught in a frantic embrace as she buried her tear-rimmed eyes on my chest and clung to me desperately as though I were the Rock of Ages.

Over her shoulder, I saw the man Enrico who had met Auriel Dodd at the airport. He came from the lift just as the car carrying Alice French started upward.

Enrico hesitated a moment beside Peter. "Seen Martinique?" he asked.

Peter shook his head negatively and grasped my elbow.

"Please hurry!" he whispered. "Enrico is looking for Martinique. He must be here." His voice was tense, his eyes worried as they followed the retreating Enrico.

CHAPTER TWO

THERE IN THE lobby I was surprised that Peter knew Alice French. The way he clutched my arm was an indication, even before he told me, that she was involved in the story in some way. I wanted to get at that story. I was anxious to heed his tense whisper to hurry away from there; why, I knew not. We were not quick enough, for as Stella unwrapped herself from me I saw dark anger mount in Peter's eyes and turned to look back toward the desk.

A man had turned toward us, a smile of satisfaction curling his thin cruel lips. I knew nothing about Martinique, had heard the name only twice, once on the boulevard as Peter cautioned me to remember the attractive building, and just a moment before when Enrico had spoken to Peter and I realized then that Martinique was a person to be feared. As the man came forward I knew he had to be Martinique. No other man could possibly have fitted the name.

He was a tall man, quite slim and exceedingly well groomed. He paused a foot or two away from us, seeming to appraise us with calculated intensity. He seemed to sway as though the air currents in the room moved him about at will. The tip of his tongue protruded from his red mouth, making me think of a swaying cobra, its fangs ready for the strike. He had uncommonly black eyes, uncommonly sharp, over a small cruel mouth with lips far too brilliantly red for a man of his age. Curious how my mind shifted from a cobra to a werewolf but that, I suppose, was because of his seemingly unholy red, blood-stained lips.

My spine revolted, cold chills encased my body. I knew instinctively I was facing the most dangerous man I had ever met. He was a man who would make very few mistakes. A man who was never held in check by any of the so-called niceties of life. A man distasteful to men but fascinating to some women. He was dangerous, evil, exciting. Any contact with him would be thrilling. I knew instinctively that he would be full of the graces and attentions dear to a woman's heart. All the cat in my nature came out as we three waited. I wanted to leap at that, to me, horrible face and scratch out and close forever those hard calculating eyes.

He seemed to enjoy Peter's discomfiture and Stella's shocked surprise. Before either he or they could speak Enrico hurried up and stepped between us, forcing Martinique to take a step backward. Enrico was annoyed, obviously displeased as he spoke in rapid Spanish to Martinique, who merely shrugged. Enrico continued but was cut short in his tirade by an emphatic, "No!" from Martinique, who then said brusquely: "I know what I am doing. Go back to the Gallery." Enrico cast a sullen look in our direction as he obeyed the command.

I wondered why we waited. My answer was the completely trapped expression on the faces of the children.

"Well, Stella, and you too, Peter, have you forgotten your manners?" he demanded as he came forward. "Welcome to Hollywood, Miss Thomas. You have stayed away too long, denying us the brilliance of your wit and the double edge of your tongue to keep us in order."

The sheer effrontery of the man made me gasp. Remembering my new name on the hotel register I drew myself up with what dignity I could muster and said acidly, "There must be some mistake. Come, children!"

"No, wait." He addressed them countermanding my order. He favored me with that thin sickening smile and said, "I just saw your card. When you registered you were either careless or just a creature of habit. You had difficulty squeezing the Stevens part of your name on the card. That told me many things, your real identity for one. Too bad you were so careless if you wanted to preserve your incognito."

"I do not care to discuss it."

"We are going to be friends, you and I," he went on.

"Not if I can help it, and I think I can," I said with emphasis. "I may be in Hollywood but I will pick my friends, Mr. . . . ." I hesitated not knowing what to call him.

"Martinique, at your service," he said, bowing as he clicked his heels together.

I wanted no contact with him and most certainly none of his service and was on the point of telling him so when I caught a slight shake of the head from Stella. "You'll excuse us," I suggested.

"Certainly," he agreed. "We have some things to discuss but you are probably tired and want to rest."

That remark annoyed me. "I'm sure we can have nothing in common, you and I."

"But we have, haven't we, Stella?"

"I suppose so," she answered, dully for her.

"Bring Miss Thomas to the Gallery, Peter." It was really a command. "She will like it there, don't you think?" He turned to me. "At the Gallery you will see many interesting and beautiful things and since you are a friend of Peter's and Stella's, the whole place will be at your disposal. My Gallery is the meeting-place for all the important people in Hollywood. You will like it. I understand, Miss Thomas, you are interested in young men. You will find them at the Gallery too. I'll see that you have an assortment to choose from."

I could have slapped him. People may say things about me and my nearly octogenarian interest in young men behind my back, but that was the first time anyone had ever dared to confront me with it in such an insulting manner. I could feel the color creeping up my neck past my collar.

While those thoughts were running through my mind Peter went into action like the gallant he was. His arm shot out, his fist caught Martinique on the chin. Martinique staggered backward under the force of the blow, his eyes full of amazed surprise to be followed by quick flashing rage. I heard astounded gasps from several people in the lobby. Peter was ready to follow through, stepping after Martinique. I loved Peter for that noble action but my joy at his behavior was short-lived as I glanced at Stella and seemed to see all light and hope die.

Martinique's hand went to his chin. I heard him say sharply, "You'll regret that blow, Peter!"

"Maybe," Peter ground out. "Don't forget there's more and harder where that one came from. I've taken all I mean to take from you, understand that?"

Behind us I heard a woman's voice say, "That handsome young lad has just committed Hollywood suicide. Who is he?"

"Some extra, I suppose," a bored voice replied.

"Come to the Gallery," Martinique retorted.

He turned on his heels and strode across the lobby. I rather fancied there were some people there who wished they had not witnessed the episode. "Why, oh, why did you do that?" Stella cried.

"You know very well why I did it, the swine," Peter replied. "Come along." He took our arms and piloted us toward the elevator.

We were all strangely silent as we rode up. Even the boy seemed impressed by the scene he had just witnessed. As a matter of fact he looked at Peter with awe.

He lighted every lamp, opened all the windows and had turned on the radio in the sitting-room before one could say Jack Robinson. I gave him a half-dollar and several sharp orders. When he left, the lights were out, the radio stilled and all but one of the windows closed. As the door shut behind him I must have turned from the dresser where I had removed my hat and adjusted my transformation with a well, what-is-it-all-about look in my eye, for Stella plunged straight to the point. There was no prelude, no preamble, just the bare words that rang through the room.

"We've killed a man," she said, "and Peter's quick fist hasn't helped us any."

So there was a dead man! I knew it from the moment Peter had said that he would kill another man. Why was there nothing in the papers about an unexplained murder? I had no time for thought because Peter cut in.

"I killed him," he claimed quickly with a defiant look in her direction. Then more gently, "Martinique insulted her, Stella."

"Let's forget that. Ethel wants the other story. I was there, Ethel. It was my fault," she insisted. "He's trying to take all the blame. It isn't fair, and there's no sense in his being so noble. Tell him so," she appealed to me.

"Don't discourage chivalry in a man. It's almost extinct these days," I warned.

"And don't you be philosophical or witty," she flashed back.

"Surely you are joking about your murder," I said. "This is some prank you have thought up to startle me so that when we come to the real explanation of your telegram I'll be glad and relieved that it is not too serious." I went through the farce of pronouncing those words but I knew by the thump of my heart and the hurt, bewildered expression in their eyes that they had told me the truth, all of it.

Peter was painfully sober. His blue-black eyes were veiled and clouded. His mouth was drawn to a taut line pulling down the sparse skin, accentuating the bony structure of his face which in repose was so perfectly formed. His head was inclined slightly forward as if to ward off an expected blow. Gone was the aristocratic, devil-may-care manner which made people, even in a crowd, turn and look at him a second time.

I moved into the sitting-room and selected a chair by the open window so that I could look down and out across the park-like grounds of the hotel. I could see the pool, a cool blue-green sparkle surrounded by sand and palm trees. Glad voices, voices in play, shrilled and laughed up at us, such a contrast to the two hurt children who faced me.

"I wish to heaven it was a joke," Peter exploded in that characteristic way of his. He had sunk into a low chair and spoke without looking up as his eyes traced the pattern in the oriental rug at his feet.

"You've got to help us, Ethel," Stella said. She moved closer to me, put a frail, finely manicured hand on my arm and looked down into my eyes.

"She's thin," I thought. "She's dieting or some other nonsense. She'll look like any one of a hundred women if she continues. And we talk of regimentation! Our women have regimented themselves to emaciated thinness, their curves have gone, their feminine charms have vanished into gaunt lines. She's killing the sweet impulsive child I knew. In a year or so that child will have vanished. She'll be a woman, no longer the Stella Wayne I knew and loved." I sighed as I considered the ravages of time.

"You will help us, won't you?" She actually bit her lips and squeezed her adorable eyes shut for a moment to hold back the tears which in spite of her Stoic effort oozed out at the corners in two crystal drops.

She was so lovely as she stood there pleading with me that I had to curb an impulse to take her into my arms and comfort her. That would have been a mistake. She was a woman facing a problem bravely, and coddling was not what she wanted. Later perhaps I could give her that too but now she wanted assurance.

Her little nose was tense with only a slight quiver at the nostrils, her mouth a firm line, her eyes clear as she watched. She threw a swift glance at Peter. In that glance I saw love and a willingness to go through hell's fire for the man she loved. Too bad he missed that glance, but then he knew that quality in her. I knew then that she would let nothing separate her from Peter—not even murder. For a moment I was assailed with doubt. Had she killed the man herself? Was Peter trying to cover up for her and take the blame? It would be just like him and that philosophy of life he had expressed when he told me that there was no one in the world who care about him or what he did.

"What we all need is a drink," I said and crossed the room. They were tense, keyed too high. I wanted them to relax.

"Not for us," Stella said as I lifted the telephone.

"Send up a bottle of good brandy, three glasses and ice," I said and replaced the receiver.

"We can count on you, can't we?" Stella asked.

"Of course. Isn't that why I am here?"

"Thank you," Peter said simply but so sincerely that I felt like crying. Stella did turn away toward the window and actually cried a few brief tears of relief.

As if there had ever been any doubt of my willingness to help her! Peter and I waited. Stella turned back from the window and said, "Sorry to be such a fool but I . . ."

There was a knock on the door. "Say nothing more until the waiter has come and gone," I warned as Peter jumped to open the door.

The waiter came in and took possession of the room. He opened the bottle and started filling the glasses with ice.

"I'll mix the drinks," I said and dug into my purse for a tip.

"Would Madame care for some soda?" he asked.

"No, but you might fill that pitcher with ice-water."

"That has been done, Madame."

"Then that is all."

He bowed himself out.

"How about you?" I asked, looking at Peter.

"I couldn't take a thing. I doubt if I'll ever drink again," he said.

"Then you were drunk when it happened," I accused.

He seemed surprised as he nodded agreement and then clasped his hands together as if in that way he would be able to hold onto himself. I glanced at Stella.

"Nothing for me," she said, and moved over to the chair to sit on the arm beside Peter, taking one of his hands in hers to hold it tenderly, protectingly. It relieved the tenseness as some vital force flowed from her to him to make him brave again as men have been reassured and made brave down through the ages by the touch of the right woman's understanding hand.

"Well, I need a drink. I don't get a shock like this every day in the week." I mixed myself a long one.

I sank back in my chair and sipped at the drink while those two tragic children waited. How could I let them down when they looked so hurt, so alone that they made my heart ache? Peter was like a man in the dock waiting for his death sentence. I wanted them to be calm before they told me the story. I wanted to get all the details without any hysterical trimmings.

"Tell me something about yourself, Peter," I suggested.

"Must we do that now?" Stella demanded.

"I want some background," I answered coldly as if her question were an affront.

She shrugged and paced up and down the room while Peter told me a little more about himself. That he was a rich young man I already knew, that he was an orphan he had told me, but I wanted to know what he was doing in Hollywood and several other things that might be important later.

"I told you I have no background," he said dully.

"You've lived, haven't you?" I asked. At his nod I went on, "How long? How? Where? What are you doing here in Hollywood?"

He smiled. "I'm a native Californian," he began. "I'm twenty-five. We were poor but respectable people until we made money in oil. That opened new fields for us. I went to college and my parents started on a trip around the world. They were killed in an airplane accident in Belgium. Their pictures and mine appeared in the local papers at the time. Mine caught the eye of a talent scout who approached me and offered me a screen test."

"So that's why you are here," I said.

"No, not exactly," he corrected. "I wanted to finish college and did. I had a diploma, I was supposedly educated but there was no place for me in business. I had thought I would like to write."

"Don't," I warned. "It gets you into all sorts of trouble."

"I never had a chance to write. I came here, called on a number of agents who wouldn't even consider giving me an interview. I recalled the name of the talent scout and went to see him. He insisted I take a screen test. I did. It opened up a new world for me. I liked it and decided I would be an actor. I started studying immediately with private instructors. I became a small cog in the studio's stock company. I had a few bit parts but nothing happened. Then I met Stella. She changed everything."

"How?" I demanded, wondering what she could have done.

"It was the miracle of meeting her, of falling in love. She gave me the spark I needed. From that day on I began getting better and better parts."

"We intended to be the Lunt and Fontanne of pictures," Stella said, her eyes glowing.

"It might have been if this tragedy had not caught up with us."

"Don't say that, Peter!" Stella cried.

"It's true."

Peter's voice dwindled away. I put my glass on the stand at my elbow and said, "Tell me all about it."

Piece by piece I got the improbable story. They both talked and I knew they were telling me the truth. They were terribly frightened and so bewildered by the events that they were blind to the one fact which was obvious to me from the start.

The day that it happened they had been working together on the same picture. They had been working late to finish their scenes. There was a young man in the cast with them, a Harold Dast. He had been friendly, seemed to know his way about town and when work was finished suggested that they go to Martinique's and perhaps win some money. Like all young people they thought it would be a lark. Eagerly they started out.

"Martinique's is the place I pointed out to you on Sunset Boulevard," Peter said. "We had never been there before. I wish to God we had stayed away."

"We didn't know," Stella said quietly.

"We knew, we heard stories about it. Of what they . . . It's supposed to be an antique shop. I guess he does sell stuff. I don't know about that. His main business is gambling and what else I . . ." He looked up at me and must have thought of what I had said about dangling sentences.

"Dast took us there, to the gambling rooms. He was well known. We had fun. We gambled. We won."

"We were gay and reckless," Stella cut in, "ready for anything. You know how it is when you are having a good time. You don't want to stop. It was Harold who suggested that we go up to his apartment for a couple of drinks."

"He lived in the apartment adjoining the gambling rooms," Peter said. "You don't know the city. The building I pointed out to you is two stories tall in the front but because of the slope of the hill it is several stories in the rear. The gambling rooms were in the rear on another street and the building in which Dast lived was down there. There's an entrance from the casino to the apartment building. Enrico, that was the man who spoke to me in the lobby, opened the door for us. You see, the apartment building made a good cover for the gambling."

"We went to Harold's apartment and drank too much," Stella admitted.

"We were fairly tight when it happened," Peter said. "We had gone beyond the danger-point."

I knew exactly what he meant. I like the taste of liquor, always have and always will, but I have never been drunk and never want to be. When I am tired, a drink picks me up. At dinners a cocktail or two breaks the ice and unties inhibitions and gives conversation a chance. At other times a highball seems to fill in the gaps, loosens tongues and ideas and when not abused is a pleasant social custom. Why it is abused I can't understand unless those of us who are weak use alcohol for an escape which in our hearts and souls we know is impossible. All people who drink too much are rarely ever excessive about other forms of food. There is only an occasional man or woman who makes a glutton of himself over dessert or meat and that man we think disgusting.

"Dast was tight too," Peter went on. "As he grew drunker his attentions to Stella increased. That made me sore."

I knew it would. One knew by looking at him that he would be a one woman man, and in spite of his protests, possessive.

"Harold became amorous." Stella took up the story without a blush. "You know how sex-conscious some men become when they are in their cups. Harold was the type. As he grew bolder and more offensive, Peter's ire rose."

"He was messy," Peter stated.

Men can be like that. I've seen it happen many a time although it is years now since a man in his cups has even considered me as anything but a nice old lady. A woman misses that. How else explain the women who should be in lavender and old lace but instead try to look younger than their grandchildren.

"I had never seen Peter jealous before," Stella said. "I suppose every woman likes to know that a man wants her alone and is willing to fight for her. The blame is really mine because I was responsible for what followed. I encouraged him just to make Peter angry."

"He didn't need encouragement," Peter denied.

"Peter wanted to leave. He had sense enough for that, but it was I who backed Harold's suggestion for just one more drink. It was that final drink that caused all the trouble. I was a fool. Peter was sulky and I . . . well, I thought I was having a good time, until Peter began to be critical. That made me contrary. I wanted to keep on annoying him. Harold had been holding my hand. He put his arm around my waist and tried to kiss me. I didn't let him do that. He grew bolder. He tried it again. Peter hit him."

"We struggled. We rolled over and over on the floor fighting it out while Stella watched," Peter said. "I didn't know what was happening until I saw a look of horror on Stella's face and realized that Harold had pulled a gun and was trying to use it."

"I couldn't move," Stella took up the narrative. "I was glued to the wall, horrified, as I realized what I had done. The fight became a frantic struggle to get the gun. They rolled over and over, first one on the top and then the other. Suddenly the advantage became Peter's, he grabbed the hand holding the gun and wrenched it free. They rose to their feet. Harold sprang at Peter. They were locked in a tight embrace. Then the gun went off. There was a deafening report, a thin wisp of smoke and the two men were suspended in space for a moment before Harold sank to the floor.

"Peter was stunned by what had happened. I saw Harold's shirt growing red with stain. I took the gun from Peter's hand and wiped it free of fingerprints. Then I bent down and pressed it into Harold's still hand. By that time Peter had started to protest. He said we must call the police but I wouldn't listen to him. I wanted to get him away from that place. I took his hand and was leading him away when our flight was halted by a voice which said, 'I believe I could use you two. You use your heads.'"

"We were panicked; I know we looked guilty," Peter said. "It was Martinique. In his hand he carried a candid camera. As we recoiled he took our picture."

"Why did he do that?" I demanded.

"Part of his plan," Peter replied gloomily. "Go on."

"While we stood there he bent down and examined Harold. He told us not to be alarmed, that it was only a flesh wound, that Harold would be all right. He promised to take care of everything."

"Why did you believe him?" I demanded.

"Because he said he didn't want any publicity so close to the gambling place. His explanations seemed logical enough at the time. We knew his reputation. He's supposed to be able to fix things in this town," Peter explained. "He promised to keep in touch with us."

Imagine the terror, if you can, of those two poor children. Peter's impulse had been the correct one. They should have notified the police of the accident immediately. Before we become too critical, let us stop and consider what we would have done in their position. Martinique had taken control of the situation. He was positive of Harold's condition, his assurance that everything would be all right, his reputation as a man who could fix things in Hollywood, his own reasons for wanting the affair kept quiet, were arguments that their numbed reason could not combat. They took his advice and fled the apartment.

They started for home but knew that sleep would be impossible. The more they thought of what had happened the more frightened they became. They needed each other. They went to Stella's, where she changed into other clothes. Then they drove over to Peter's apartment. After that, they drove about for the rest of the night. In the morning they went back to the apartment and insisted upon seeing Martinique. The card he had given them made that possible. After a long delay he appeared. He told them he had had a busy night. He said Harold had taken a bad turn and had died from a sudden and unexpected hemorrhage.

That news, of course, took the world from under their feet and left them suspended in space. When they recovered from the first shock of the news they thanked him valiantly for what he had done and said that they would notify the police and assume all responsibility for what had happened.

Imagine their surprise when Martinique curtly told them that such a procedure was impossible. To their arguments he replied that any report they made to the police would of necessity involve him, that such a return for the help he had offered was not the reward he expected, that in his effort to help them he had involved himself in a situation that would bring harm and disgrace, probably ruin his business, that since no one knew about the affair he had taken steps, had disposed of the body, that everything would be all right, that there was no need for them to worry further, that everything had been fixed. He had ended by saying coldly, "Forget it ever happened. One extra, more or less, in Hollywood will never be missed."

To sit there and hear that story was like reading some wild improbable tale in a book or watching a film in the theatre that did not ring quite true. My senses and reason kept saying, "It isn't true, it can't be true," and yet when I looked at their drawn tired faces, poor dears, I knew they had been telling me the truth.

"And then what happened?" I asked.

"I wired you as soon as Martinique refused to talk to us again," Stella said. "That's all, so far."

"We haven't eaten, haven't slept. What are we going to do? Should we go to the police? Would it be fair now to involve Martinique in this thing?" Peter was beside himself.

"Where's the body?" I asked.

"We don't know," Peter replied.

"Smart man, Martinique," I commented, which jerked them to swift attention. "You can't go to the police because if you do Martinique will deny your story. He has no intention of becoming involved. He has made sure of his own position by tying your hands. You are quite helpless."

"But I can't live with this thing hanging over my head wondering where the body is, when it will be found and if someone will remember that we were the last people to be seen with him that night. I'm beginning to get the jitters already. Every time I see a cop or hear a police siren I think they are after me. I've got to do something or go mad. Now I know what is meant by a guilty conscience."

"Wait, Peter!" Stella's voice pleaded. "Don't you see what Ethel means? We can't prove anything unless we know what Martinique did with the body. You can't walk into a police station and say I killed a man and then expect them to go hunt for the body, not with Martinique mixed up in the thing."

Peter was seeing all the dark side of it and argued, "But when they realize that Harold is missing, when they start investigating, when they learn that he was with us that night, what are we going to do then?"

"For the moment remember that 'they' do not exist. Is there any reason for an investigation? How many people know that you were together?" I asked.

"Martinique knows."

"And Martinique does not want to talk. Don't worry about that angle," I advised.

"Do you mean that you want us to sit here and do nothing, say nothing?" he demanded in shocked amazement.

"I want you to think. I want time to think myself. You wounded a man, you didn't kill him. You shot him in self-defense which is not a crime. Unfortunately he did die of the injury. You have done no heinous thing. You did, however, make a mistake, you listened to Martinique. If it were not for him, you would have nothing to worry about except the publicity. Since Martinique is involved we must think of something to do. How many pictures did he take?"

"I don't know. I only remember one flash. Why do you suppose he did that?" Peter asked.

"I've no idea," I answered truthfully. "Why he had a camera with him in the first place baffles me and why he wanted the picture I can't imagine unless he wanted to protect himself." My mind was racing ahead of my words exploring the possibilities of the situation.

"What do you really think?" Stella asked practically.

"That we need time, that you two need a bracer. You must be hungry too. I'll have some sandwiches sent up." I went to the telephone and gave the order.

"Get lots of coffee," Peter suggested.

I knew that was a good sign. When a man begins to think of his stomach his troubles are not pressing him as hard as they might be.

The telling of the story had relaxed them both, robbed them of the tension under which they had lived for two days. I thought about it as I watched them eat the sandwiches and drink the strong black coffee. It all could have happened just as they related it. If all of the story was true why had Martinique said and done the things that he did? There was something radically wrong about the whole thing. I couldn't put my finger on it then but I knew there was a nigger in the woodpile somewhere. It was not that I didn't believe the children. I did. But their story had overtones, angles they were unaware of, facets that needed explanation. I knew they were in serious trouble, how serious I had no means of knowing at the time. I was not worried even then by the possible homicide charge that might eventually be brought home to Peter. I suppose it was my intuition or just a woman's suspicious nature that sensed something more than appeared on the surface.

"How well do you know Martinique?" I asked.

"Not well. . . . That is, I don't. Stella has been hobnobbing with him."

"I have not," Stella said defensively. "I've met him at parties, I've been polite to him. It's the thing to do. He's been very attentive lately, rather too friendly," she admitted.

"You've been extra nice to him," Peter accused. As a light flamed in Stella's eyes he said, "I'm not criticizing you. You'd like to get the part of Annabella—what actress wouldn't?"

"He's right," Stella admitted; "I've been playing up to Martinique for purely professional reasons."

"Have you tried to see him since the tragedy?"

Stella nodded. "But I haven't seen him—he won't see me either."

"He wants something," I stated. "What?"

"Stella," Peter replied bluntly.

I looked to Stella for a denial, but none shone in her eyes. She believed Peter's statement. I had no desire to press the matter further right then. They were tired and overwrought. I didn't want them to quarrel.

"What do you know about Harold Dast?" I asked to change the subject.

"Not much," Peter replied.

"Good heavens!" I exclaimed and then lest they consider my explosion exasperation I went on: "How long have you known him?"

"Just the two days we worked on the picture, which is a lifetime in Hollywood," Peter explained.

"But—" I began a protest.

He laughed goodnaturedly. Some of that easy grace was returning to him. "You don't understand how fast or slow life can be in this town. It is a little like living on shipboard. You meet people, know them intimately for a short time, hear their dreams, their hopes and their desires. You rub elbows with them with the ease of old friends. The man you see today is the man you are apt to see tomorrow until something steps in to separate you or change the direction of your life. It may be a job on location. You are gone for a few days. When you return the people you knew are doing something different, or just busy, your close contact is gone. It's quite as if you had never known them at all."

"In this lifelong friendship of two days, just what did you learn about him, his hopes, and dreams?" I asked sarcastically.

"Not much and a great deal. He's from the East. Has always been interested in the theatre. Did theatrical work at Harvard, acted in summer stock, had a few small parts on Broadway and then decided to try pictures. He was doing rather well for a beginner."

"What about his family?"

"He mentioned his mother. Said she never understood him. They didn't get on at all. She is a wealthy woman and wanted him to live her life rather than have a life of his own. He said his coming out here was an open revolt. She cut off his allowance but he was determined to prove to her that he could make his own way and did not need or want her pampering influence."

"And where is his mother now?" I asked. I wanted to know all the possible obstacles to our progress.

"In the East, I think," he replied.

"Then let us hope she stays there for a little while," I said.

Peter put down his coffee cup and looked across at me. "Your reactions are not at all what I expected. You puzzle me."

"That's because I am puzzled. This is not an easy problem you have presented."

"Don't worry about Ethel," Stella said brightly. "She's been thinking. I've been watching her, could almost hear the wheels go round."

"But we don't want her to become involved in this," he said. "It's bad enough as it is. Look here! I even have the key to Harold's apartment." He had been fingering coins in his pocket just before he held out the key.

"How on earth did you get that?" I asked, trying to conceal the pleasure I had derived from the statement.

"He handed it to me when we went in the other night. I unlocked the door and forgot to return it. I don't want to keep it and I don't know what to do with it."

"Just put it on the tray," I suggested. "I'll dispose of it."

The key rattled down to the tray, clinking against a saucer.

"Any advice to offer?" he asked, and yawned.

"Just this. Don't you worry about me. I'm already involved in this case. I'm condoning a criminal action, withholding information from the police and enjoying it. We'll all be in it deeper than we are now before we are out of it, so forget that. I've trifled with the police before, and I'll do it again if I live long enough. It's not what you do that counts against you but what they catch you doing."

That was, I realized, a rather garbled quotation from something written by Oscar Wilde. I wondered if it had been written bitterly after his experience or if it was something his agile mind had thought of before, or if perhaps he had lifted it from some other and earlier writer. The more I read the more I realize that modern authors are repeatedly repeating the quips and wise remarks of the ancients and offering them as their very own. Of course they have a first-rate precedent to follow—Shakespeare did it all the time.

Relaxation and food had had its effect. They were both yawning and I realized that Peter, particularly, was dead from lack of sleep. Much of the hunted fear had gone from their tired faces.

"You need some sleep, you two," I suggested.

"Couldn't do it," Peter protested.

"I'm afraid you must. Go into the bedroom, Stella," I suggested. "I'll make Peter comfortable here." He was reluctant to stretch out on the couch, but after Stella had gone he did lie back. In a few moments his long legs were making soft dents in the cushions. I waited. He had fallen asleep almost instantly. I went to the bedroom and came back with a blanket. I removed his shoes and covered him. I closed the Venetian blinds that had been making a slatted pattern of golden sunlight on the floor. I then took the key to Harold Dast's apartment and slipped it into the pocket of my skirt.

Stella was stretched across my bed and said sleepily as I went in, "It was good of you to come, Ethel."

"You knew I'd come. Don't go to sleep until I have had a chance to talk to you. What do you know about Martinique that Peter only suspects?"

Her eyes jerked open in surprise. "What did he tell you?" She sat up wide awake.

"He fears something that you might do and I rather guess it has to do with Martinique."

"It does. Martinique wants me to become his mistress."

"He what?"

"You heard me, Ethel, and you're not shocked either," she retorted.

"But why?"

"Because I'm young and attractive, I suppose," she said.

"And what do you think about the proposition?" I demanded.

"I laughed at it until the other night. Now, I don't know," she said thoughtfully, slowly.

"But it's ridiculous. Things aren't done that way any more," I protested. "Of course, you are attractive but there are thousands of attractive young women in Hollywood who would jump at the chance if it meant advancement in pictures. Would it?"

"That was what he told me. Promised me all sorts of things," she replied.

"And his proposition, was it made before this Dast business?"

"Yes. He knows I'm up for a big part, one I'd very much like to play. He has power out here, Ethel. I guess he knows where more than one body is buried." She stopped and turned startled eyes toward me. "Ethel, you heard what I just said! It was only a catch-phrase, but do you suppose . . ."

"I'm not supposing. All I know is this: Martinique, at the moment, thinks he has you in his power, Peter too." I wasn't prepared to tell her what I actually thought of the story she and Peter had told me. I didn't really know myself. It was just the germ of an idea then. His mistress indeed! Stella was not that glamorous. In a place like Hollywood, full of the most beautiful girls in the world, her statement simply did not make sense. I've found that a man's passion fluctuates with the supply and demand.

"He has us where he wants us. We can't deny that fact," she said.

"But he has made a mistake," I reminded her. "With Dast out of the way he can prove nothing. He has been depending on your fear, and fear alone, if he has had an ulterior motive for what he has done."

"That's right, he has. He's as much in our power as we are in his, isn't he? Suppose he does threaten us, we can defy him, can't we?" There was a trace of hope in her voice.

"Yes, but don't forget that he could send that photograph to the police anonymously and get you into trouble. The burden of all proof would be on your shoulders if he did such a thing," I warned her.

"It's a mess."

"And if you don't want it made worse, keep away from Martinique," I cautioned. "Peter told me he would kill another man if you did something and now I know what he meant."

"Poor Peter. I love him so, Ethel."

"I know and he loves you, so be careful. Lie back and take a nap. I have a few errands I want to do. I'm going out now but I'll be back in time for a cocktail."

"I can't let anything happen to Peter," she said, and closed her eyes. After a moment she asked without opening them, "Is virtue an overrated commodity?"

"Don't talk nonsense!"

"Why do men set so much store by a woman's virtue and neglect their own?" She was mumbling, more than half asleep, but knowing the stock from which she sprang I was afraid of what she might do.

Peter was sprawled out like a Great Dane and snoring lustily as I crossed to the phone and put in a call for New York.

My friend Inspector Conklin of the New York police was interested and eager for information, but I told him nothing, simply asked him to get some information for me. He wanted to be helpful, even suggested getting in touch with Inspector Duncan of the Los Angeles police, an old friend of his, but I discouraged that at once. In fact, I made him promise that no matter what happened he would forget that he had ever heard my name connected with that of Harold Dast. There was a chuckle in his warm Irish voice as he gave his promise and the line went dead.

Peter was making a terrific din. Sawing wood, I believe that particular brand of snoring is called. I thought of poor Stella and the sleepless nights ahead of her, of what she would have to endure in the way of nocturnal noises but I suppose if you care for a man enough to sleep with him you are able to put up with his noises.

I left them to their slumbers. As I carefully closed the door the key to Harold Dast's apartment jiggled in my pocket.

CHAPTER THREE

I HAD NO DEFINITE plan as I left the hotel. My first impulse was to go directly to the Dast apartment and have a look at it, but I changed my mind about that. There were so many things I wanted to see and know, and of paramount importance was the man Martinique. I wanted to see him before he could put into operation some retaliation for the blow Peter had given him. I called a cab and told the driver to take me to Martinique's.

The Gallery was a charming building but there was something about its interior that depressed me the moment I passed by the elaborately dressed attendant at the door. The main room was large and might have been a beautiful drawing-room if properly handled. Every piece of furniture was for sale and had been arranged to tempt the possible buyer, but it was not the obvious commercial tone of the place that spoiled its effect. There were old crystal chandeliers shedding soft light on rich mahogany and rosewood. Cabinets against the walls were filled with silver, china and glass.

It was very beautiful and breath-taking, my first glimpse of it, but that impression lasted only a moment. The gorgeous flowers—long spikes of delphinium, calla-lilies, snapdragons and pungent stock massed in profusion everywhere—would have given the place an air of gaiety had it not been for the heavy, sickening scent of tuberoses. That smell so reminiscent of family funerals made the whole room repulsive.

It was just the touch I would expect a man like Martinique to use.

Opposite the main entrance there was an archway leading to a wide foyer. As I moved into the foyer I was confronted by a large mahogany desk behind which sat a dark, hard-bitten woman. She wore severely tailored clothes, a white shirtwaist, plain black earrings as hard and cold as her impersonal eyes which were studying me. A good watchdog, I thought as I noted the wooden block on her desk which informed me that I was facing Miss Alvera.

I gave my name as Stevens and told her I wanted to see Mr. Martinique.

When I was finally ushered into his office I was immediately repelled by the same heavy scent of tuberoses which there mingled with the sweet pungency of a huge bowl of floating gardenias.

As he rose from his desk I noted with satisfaction that a red welt still showed the effectiveness of Peter's blow. Enrico was with him, sitting in the chair at the end of the desk. Enrico turned to face me.

"Miss Thomas, my assistant Enrico." I bowed an acknowledgment of the introduction. With that way he had of ignoring a person Martinique continued in explanation to Enrico: "Miss Thomas insists upon playing her little game of pretending to be Miss Stevens. She does not know us, does she?"

"Perhaps you underrate me," I suggested.

"Which would be foolish of me, wouldn't it?" he said with his thin smile which assured me that he was quite sure of himself.

"Does your assistant know all your business?" I asked bluntly.

"I have no secrets from Enrico."

"Then I will be brief. I have heard the children's story and came to tell you that you have no hold over them, that we do not propose to be blackmailed by you in any way, that you can give the part of Annabella to Auriel Dodd or any other actress you like. Stella is not interested and will not be your mistress."

I thought I saw Enrico's eyes spark at that. Martinique shrugged. "Perhaps you are underestimating me."

"Not at all. I'm quite sure that you are capable of anything. The Dast episode proves that. Just what you plan to do, why you are dangling this part before the eyes of so many women, I do not know, nor do I know or understand your power in this city and your seeming control of the motion-picture industry—unless, of course, it is blackmail."

"That is an unfortunate word, Miss Thomas."

"I quite agree with you. It is a nasty word and all things connected with it are quite horrible, particularly the fear of your victims. I have convinced the children that their safest course is to tell the truth and devil take the consequences."

"You are making a mistake," Enrico said promptly.

"I can take care of this," Martinique said quickly, scowling at Enrico.

"You have bungled it," Enrico accused. "What is this woman doing here? How does she know so much of our plans? What gives her the courage to speak this way?"

"You do not understand, Enrico. It is part of the plan. Miss Thomas does not know our power. She speaks in ignorance."

"She is a blind fool. She can spoil everything," Enrico retorted.

"I think not," Martinique assured him. "Go attend to your business. I can take care of Miss Thomas."

Enrico stalked from the room, an enraged man. "How do you propose to block my plans?" Martinique asked.

"I'll let you guess about that," I retorted. "I came to warn you that we mean to fight."

"You didn't come here to tell me that."

"True," I admitted. "I came to see you in your proper setting so that I could properly gage you. These things, are they all for sale?" I nodded toward a cabinet, trying to show him that further conversation was unnecessary.

He was willing to follow my lead, seemed relieved.

"Certainly. I'll have a clerk show you about if you like."

"No, I never deal with underlings," I replied crisply.

"You are a wise woman."

"That's as may be but don't try to flatter me."

"Sit down," he invited. "I'd like to show you some of my treasures. I can see that you are a woman of appreciation. This can be an interlude in our affairs."

I took the chair at the end of the desk while he opened a cabinet. He brought several things for me to inspect. The man baffled me. While we were both playing a game his indifference, either real or assumed, was annoying. He held a small vase cupped lovingly in his long pointed fingers. He moved some papers aside to find a place for it. It was then that I spied the bracelet. I lost interest in everything else. My mother had had a pair of old gold bracelets which I had always wanted, but they went to my older sister and then on down the line to her children. The one I picked up from the partly opened drawer at my elbow was an exquisite thing and quite like our family heirloom.

"Do you have the mate to this?" I asked eagerly, ignoring the vase.

The man was startled. For the fraction of a second, I had caught him off guard. His eyes were steady as he looked at me and said smoothly, "Sorry, but that is not for sale. It was left by a client for a slight repair. See," he said, "the catch is loose." He took it from my hand and dropped it back into the drawer.

I knew there was nothing the matter with the bracelet but I was willing to play his game. "If your client would consider selling the pair, get in touch with me. I'm not interested in anything else at the moment." I stood up. "I think I'll play a little roulette."

"So you are a gambler."

"Aren't we all?"

While he carefully replaced the vase in its cabinet I had a chance to study the room. His desk was in the far corner and nearly opposite the door by which I had entered. In the rear wall of the room there was a door which I was to learn led to a hall, an angle of the foyer from which I had just come. The room was exquisitely paneled in light mahogany. Behind me there was a door which might have opened into the gallery proper but I knew from the arrangement of the showrooms in the gallery that this must be a closet.

He crossed from a cabinet to a section of the rear wall and pressed his fingers against the molding. One of the panels slid open revealing a small lift. With a wave of his hand he invited me to enter.

At that moment the door from the foyer was thrown violently open and Auriel Dodd, fire in her eyes, burst into the room. "What's this talk about giving the part of Annabella to Stella Wayne?" she demanded.

"You've been listening to gossip," he said.

"I've heard it too," I said quickly.

"Now, you look here, Martinique, I'm willing to play your game just so far. I don't need you. I have a reputation in New York. I can go back there. Do I get that part or not?" She was perfect as she stood there, face flushed, eyes aflame, fully dramatizing the moment.

"You cannot force my hand, Auriel," he said quietly.

"I didn't come out here blind to your tricks. Just don't forget that I know a thing or two, enough to upset your apple cart," she warned.

At the door I saw Enrico obviously enjoying the situation.

"Sit down, calm yourself until I return. And you, Enrico, close the door. I will deal with you later."

"Enrico didn't tell me," she said a little too quickly for conviction.

"Perhaps it was a little bird. We shall see."

The door to the foyer closed. "And now, Miss Thomas, I will take you down since you want to gamble, but I warn you, it is dangerous to play your stakes against Martinique. I like to know the weaknesses of my enemies."

"Aren't you flattering yourself?" I asked.

"Do you mean that you want to be my friend?" he asked brazenly.

"Hardly." I stepped into the lift leaving Auriel Dodd completely deflated as she watched us go.

We rode down in silence. When the lift stopped and the door slid open he offered a hand to help me out but I shrank away. "You are making a mistake in your attitude," he warned. His voice was like velvet as his eyes darted about the room.

Across from us I saw Enrico coming down the stairs. I felt like saying "Scat!" to Martinique, putting an end to the silly situation.

"I think we understand each other. We should be friends, you and I," he suggested.

"I'm particular about my friends," I retorted. "I don't associate with blackmailers."

"Is that a threat?"

"You ought to know. I still believe in the police."

He smiled annoyingly and beckoned Enrico, saying, "Miss Thomas wants to try her luck. See that she gets a good seat at a roulette table." He clicked his heels, bowed, stepped back into the lift. "Until we meet again," he said as the panel slid between us.

Enrico bowed quite as if I were a stranger. He was swarthy, probably a Mexican. I had been interested in his round face, utterly void of expression except for his liquid brown eyes, which at the moment were focused just over my head. His skin was smooth and soft, his mouth firm. Not a muscle of that face moved as he waited for me to step forward. In spite of his lack of expression I knew he thoroughly disapproved of me.

There was more activity in the salon than I had expected to find at that hour of the afternoon. I selected a seat which commanded a view of the lift and the stairs which I felt sure must lead to the foyer outside of Martinique's office.

The room was breathlessly quiet as the players devoted their attention to losing their money. At a nearby table I could hear a blackjack player say, "Hit me again." Down the room I heard the click of dice and the murmuring voices of men wooing their points. At the roulette tables the croupiers' hollow announcements followed the spinning of the wheel and the rattle of the tumbling ball.

The play was not exciting. I won too easily. As I raked in and arranged pile after pile of chips I wondered if Martinique had in some way told Enrico to let me win. I don't know how a wheel is "fixed" but I don't trust any of them and I didn't believe in my luck to the extent of my winnings. I chuckled. It was going to be a good joke on Martinique. I would never play in his place again. Just to see how far they would go I placed five hundred in the center of four numbers.

The wheel was spun, the ball was dropped. My turbulent thoughts raced with it. One look about that lavish room convinced me that Martinique had ample police protection. He, therefore, was not worried about my police threat. I felt confident of one thing, however— Martinique would not want the story publicized; blackmailers never want the truth to be known. I smiled inwardly. The man was a little afraid of me. Let him wonder what my next move would be. In the meantime, he would set a trap for me if he could. I felt quite satisfied that he did not expect me to go to Dast's apartment.

The spinning ball was beginning to make clicking sounds prior to falling. It dropped. I won. The croupier, his face a frozen mask, pushed four thousand dollars in chips across the table. New bets were placed, the wheel was spun.

"It's a dirty racket!" The words exploded from a woman sitting across the table as she eyed my chips enviously. Poor soul, she had been placing each bet as if life itself depended on the outcome. She had smoked incessantly, lighting each cigarette with nervous fingers as her eyes rotated with the wheel.

Enrico was at her side almost immediately and took hold of her arm.

"Take your filthy hands off me!" She jerked her arm away from him and leaning forward said, "You'd better put that roll in your sock, Grandma, and stay the hell away from here. They'll get you if you come back. You'll never win again!"

"I think Madame had better stop playing," Enrico said persuasively. His voice seemed to come from behind a mask.

With a defeated hopeless shrug she rose from the table and sauntered away, pretending to ignore Enrico's threatening eyes.

I went on playing, placing smaller bets. I won and lost but I kept my four thousand as a substantial reserve. Sometime later I was conscious of someone standing behind me. It was the woman who had lost so much money. "This is no place for you unless you are lousy with money," she said. "Take it from me, I know!"

I glanced up. Her eyes were wistfully roving over my large stack of chips. "Could I make you a loan?" I asked.

"It wouldn't do any good. I'd lose it. I . . ."

"You must not annoy the players," Enrico's crisp voice cut into the conversation.

"All right, all right," she said. She moved away beside Enrico. Her voice was pitched in hysteria. "I want to see Martinique!"

Enrico led her across the room and pressed a button in the paneled wall. The panel slid back, the woman stepped in. Enrico turned back into the room, his attention drawn to a group at the foot of the stairs. A man was arguing with two flunkies. He was insisting that he had to see Martinique. He wrenched his arms free from the men who held him. His fists were clenched, he was ready to fight.

Enrico was a born diplomat. I could not hear what they said but in a moment Enrico and the man were on their way to the lift. They disappeared behind the panel.

I was wondering about that lift. Surely Martinique didn't want wild women and infuriated men barging into his private office. It did not seem reasonable, or at all like him.

Down the table I heard a girl mutter behind the cigarette which hung loosely in her lips, "If they don't want to lose their dough, why don't they stay the hell away from here?"

"Maybe his wife lost the rent," a companion suggested as her carmine-tipped fingers dropped chips on the board.

"I been watching that old girl. She's in a winning streak."

"I been doing all right," the first one said.

"She's new, ain't she?" the second one asked with a glance in my direction.

"Yeah, never seen her before. Funny-looking old girl, ain't she. Looks as if she stepped out of a storybook."

"It's probably a gag. You know what this town is. She'll attract attention in that rig. Looks like a fugitive from *Gone With the Wind*, don't she?"

They were completely oblivious to the fact that I might hear them. I paid no attention but went on with my play for a few minutes, watching them both. They tried to duplicate my bets. Bored, I cashed in my chips and prepared to leave.

Enrico met me at the lift, his smooth dead-pan crinkled by an attempt at a smile. "Has Madame been lucky?"

"Very," I replied, as I fingered the key to Harold Dast's apartment.

"Are you going back to the gallery?" he asked.

"Is there any other way?" I asked innocently.

I could only imagine that his eyes were hard and doubting as he replied, "You must have heard of the exit through the adjoining building."

I had seen people come and go through that exit. As I fingered Dast's key I made up my mind to see Martinique again, have it out with him. As I had played I had convinced myself of one point in connection with the children's story. My conviction had to be true. I'd face him with the fact and that, I was sure, would end our connection with Martinique. "I'll go up the stairs," I said.

"Very well." He bowed as I walked away.

When I reached the top of the stairs I was, as I had expected to be, in the foyer just outside of Martinique's office. Miss Alvera was not at her desk. I tried the handle to Martinique's door but it was locked. I wandered out into the gallery looking for someone. The place seemed strangely deserted. I walked to the front door where the livened doorman watched the humming traffic.

I saw something that gave me a bad shock. There could be no mistake about it nor could there be another car like that cream-colored creation of Peter's. It was parked at the curb just a few feet away from the entrance.

What was Peter doing at Martinique's when I had left him sleeping in my sitting-room at the hotel? I'd find out. I didn't want him there. Why didn't he leave things to me? Why did he have to make matters worse? Really annoyed at Peter, I turned.

It certainly was a day for unexpected happenings, for coming toward me was the last person in the world I had expected to see. Henrietta Wayne bore down on me, a tragic iceberg adrift in a sea of corruption.

"Well, Ethel, at last! Where have you been?" the demanded with frigid annoyance.

"Just out," I replied. "Fancy meeting you here"

"Don't be facetious, Ethel. This is no time for levity. I know all about it," she said tragically.

"About what?" I parried.

"You know perfectly well what I mean. This horrible mess of Stella's. What are we going to do?"

"I'm sure I don't know. Who told you?"

"Of course, I was the last one to know. I can't see why Stella sent for you when I was right here to give her advice."

"I'm not so sure it was or is advice she needs," I replied crisply. When Henrietta becomes the injured mother, she tries my patience to the limit.

"But think of the scandal!" Henrietta wailed.

"Scandal be damned! The life and happiness of those two children are more to be considered."

"It's this terrible moving-picture business, this horrible place. Why should a daughter of mine do this sort of thing?"

"Maybe being your daughter is the reason. Now stop wailing and tell me what brought you here."

"That horrible man, that Martinique," she snapped. "And think of it, Ethel, I had to sit there and listen to his proposition, had to sit there knowing I was powerless to act."

"What proposition?" I demanded quickly.

"Don't you know?" Her tones scorched me. "He wants to marry Stella."

"Marry her! Tell me what he said," I urged.

"He said he asked me to come—he really ordered me to come—to give my consent to his marriage with Stella. Can you imagine it?"

"Why not? Stella is a very attractive girl."

"Don't be difficult, Ethel. You know all about this horrible killing. He told me, ordered me, to persuade Stella to marry him."

"And are you going to do it?" I demanded.

"I don't know."

"You ought to know. Can't you forget the Social Register long enough to realize what such a thing would do to Stella's life? If she were my daughter I'd rather see her dead!" I stormed.

"I'd rather see him dead." Henrietta bit the words out at me with one of the first genuine displays of feeling I had ever seen her have.

"Now you're talking," I approved. "Where are the children?"

"I don't know. Stella has been looking for Peter and Peter has been looking for Stella."

"So I'll go look for both of them," I said and left her.

When I returned to the foyer Miss Alvera was not at her post but the door to Martinique's office was open. I went in. The office was empty. I went to the wall and pressed the molding as I had seen him do earlier in the afternoon. The panel slid open. The lift was there. I started down to the gambling room.

I think my appearance was something of a shock to Enrico, but he made no comment. I went through the room thoroughly, hoping to find Peter, Stella or both. I didn't know whether to return by the stairs or take the lift and decided that I had had enough climbing for one day. Enrico preceded me to the lift and pressed the button.

He opened the door for me and was a bit startled—I know I was—when Stella popped out. The door slid shut, the lift started up. Before she could say a word, I took her arm and led her toward the stairs.

"Where's Peter?" she asked anxiously.

"I don't know, but I have seen your mother."

"She told me."

"Why did you come here, either of you?" I asked.

"When I woke up after a short nap, I went out into the sitting-room. You were both gone. I asked the doorman if he had seen either of you. He told me that you had come here, that Peter had been asking about you and had driven away. Ethel, we're in an awful mess."

"Does Peter know that Martinique wants to marry you?"

"I haven't seen him."

"Why did Peter come here?" I asked.

"Because he's like a small boy who has to take his fire-engine apart to see how it works. He always wants to know why about everything. His car is outside but I haven't been able to find him. Martinique swears that Peter hasn't been in to see him. Where can he be? What is he doing? It's probably something crazy. He may be trying to find the body."

"What body?" I asked.

"You know, Harold."

I cautioned her to be quiet as we reached the top of the stairs.

Stella marched across the foyer and stopped before Miss Alvera to demand, "Where is Peter Bradley?"

"I don't know. I told you that before," she barked. She seemed agitated. I had not expected to see her display so much emotion. She turned to me. "You're Miss Thomas, aren't you?" At nod she complained. "I've been trying to find you. Martinique wants to see you."

"And I want to see him."

While I spoke she pressed a key and said into a talk-a-phone, "Miss Thomas is here now."

I left a surprised Stella behind me as I went into Martinique's office. What on earth could he want so soon? Where had he been just a moment before?

Auriel Dodd was sitting beside Martinique's desk. She was more composed than she had been before. She looked up and gave me her best professional smile. "Good-afternoon," I said curtly.

"You know each other?" Martinique pretended surprise.

"We were in the same plane," I answered. "What did you want?"

"A little matter of business," he replied. "I'm going to need your help."

"And you are not going to get it," I said tersely. "I'd rather see Stella Wayne dead than married to you."

He actually frowned. Auriel Dodd's reactions were entirely different. My statement had given her a terrible jolt, but I give her due credit. After the first shock she covered her feelings cleverly. She favored Martinique with a cold hard stare.

He was trapped. I had not expected to put him to so much discomfort. He looked from me to Auriel as he said, "Who suggested such an improbable idea to you?"

"You suggested it to Mrs. Wayne," I stated flatly.

"I think I'll run along, Marty," Auriel purred, and gathered several yards of silver fox in preparation for her going. She was all cat as she looked down at him.

"But I want to talk to you," he objected.

"Is there anything you can say—now?" she asked.

"A great deal. Go down, try your luck. I'll see you in half an hour."

Auriel shrugged. With a poisonous nod in my direction, she stepped into the lift.

"There is never a dull moment when you are about, is there?" he asked. "Do you always say the wrong thing?"

"I say what is in my mind," I snapped.

"A habit which can be dangerous," he warned.

"Come, come, man. I'm not here for polite conversation. Why were you trying to contact me? I just saw you."

"Business. I want to take over your contract. I want to handle your career out here."

"And I don't want you," I retorted.

"And you have no respect for me or my power in this town? Is that what I am to infer?" he asked.

"Neither you nor your power. Infer anything you like," I retorted.

"I'll show you." He used the talk-a-phone. "Has Flannigan arrived? . . . Send him in!"

I had stood up. "I'm not interested in your ability to prove a point which does not interest me." I declared. There was no doubt about it, the man could be most irritating.

The door opened. A tall man, ruddy of complexion, with bright blue eyes and a warm smile, stepped inside.

"Ah, Flannigan," Martinique purred. "This is Miss Ethel Thomas." He sat back, amusement in his eyes at Flannigan's surprise.

Flannigan's friendly face expanded into a warm smile. "Miss Thomas, eh? Say, what do you mean sneaking into Hollywood without letting us hear a word about it?" Before I could reply he went on, "I'm Tim Flannigan, your agent. You certainly helped us put over a nice deal. Glad to know you. Are you ready to go to work tomorrow?"

"No, next week," I answered, a little breathless because of his haste.

"You might as well begin drawing down the shekels," he advised with a laugh.

"Next week will be soon enough," I insisted.

Martinique cut into the conversation. "Miss Thomas and I have been having a little conversation. I have decided that she is in the wrong hands. She is to be my client from now on."

"What?" Flannigan gasped.

"Pay no attention to him, Mr. Flannigan. I wouldn't be a client of his," I sputtered.

Martinique ignored my statement and said, "You'll arrange to have Miss Thomas's contract transferred to me in the morning."

"And I say, do not do it, Mr. Flannigan. Do you understand?" I demanded.

Poor Flannigan, angry and a little bewildered, was caught between the two of us.

"And I say do it," Martinique snapped.

Flannigan leaned over the desk and glowered down at Martinique. His face was red, his fighting Irish blood was warming up. "You can't do this to me, Martinique! I'll tear your heart out!" he cried. He reached a great fist across the desk and caught Martinique by the lapels of his coat.

I shouldn't have minded if Flannigan had carried out his threat; in fact, I was rather hoping he would. I wanted to see Martinique hurt.

"You're forgetting something, Flannigan." The words shot from between Martinique's too-red lips.

Flannigan was lifting him out of his chair. "You'll pay for this."

"Don't let him bluff you, Mr. Flannigan," I urged.

My voice seemed to break the spell. Tim released his grip. Martinique's body returned to the chair with a thud. With a composure that was only assumed Martinique brushed his lapels where Flannigan's hands had been. Flannigan turned to me with pained eyes and a mouth quivering with shame. "I can't help myself," he said, and tumbled toward the door where Miss Alvera watched with amusement and satisfaction in her hard, cruel eyes.

"You see how it is," Martinique said. "From now on you are in my hands."

"One of us will be dead first," I threatened, and went to the door. I gave that she-devil Alvera a wicked thrust out of my way.

That round had definitely gone to Martinique. I was furious. I stopped, returned to the desk and leaning forward, said, "I want that picture you took the other night, murderer!" He actually shrank away from me. "I'll give you ten minutes to give it to me. I'll be back." I started toward the door again. "Remember," I threatened, "in ten minutes or you take the consequences!"

I was excited as I entered the foyer. Flannigan was barging toward the front entrance. "Mr. Flannigan!" I called, and hurried after him. He must have heard me but he didn't stop. I picked up my long skirts and started running. "Wait!" I called.

I caught him as he yanked at the door. "Wait," I begged.

"I want to get out of this hell hole," he growled.

"Isn't that what he wants you to do?" I asked.

"How can you talk to me after what you have just seen?" he demanded. "I'm ashamed of myself; I should think you'd be ashamed to be seen talking to me."

"Easy, man," I cautioned. "Come back! Don't run away admitting you're whipped."

"You saw me take my whipping, aren't you satisfied?" he cried.

"No. I'm not going to be a client of his. You're not going to turn my contract over to him. I have a little score to settle with him myself. If you transfer that contract you'll be delivering me into his hands. You wouldn't do that, would you?"

"No."

"You've got to fight him. If you quit now you're licked for all time. You don't want to go on dancing when he pulls the strings, do you?" I demanded.

"No, but . . ."

"I know—you're afraid of something. Can he expose you without hurting himself a little?" I asked pointedly.

"Not very well. Say! What have you done?"

"Nothing yet but I need help, your help. Go in there and tell him you won't transfer the contract."

"By God, I will!" He squared his shoulders. "Say, you're all right."

There was a light of battle in Flannigan's eyes as he retraced his steps. I felt quite satisfied with myself. We had Martinique where we wanted him. As soon as that picture was in my hands I would call Inspector Duncan. In the meantime, Flannigan would assert his manhood, gain back some of his lost confidence. He would no longer feel whipped and ashamed.

I looked for Henrietta. I went in and out of all the little display rooms that lined the rear of the shop. She was nowhere in sight. What a mix-up! Stella was looking for Peter, I had started out to find them both. I had thought Henrietta would have sense enough to wait for us, but no, not Henrietta.

It was late afternoon. The gallery was eerily quiet. I went to the archway. Miss Alvera was at her desk. There was no sign of life in the place at all. Outside on the walk the doorman stood at the curb watching the traffic. Why didn't they come? I wanted to get away from the place.

The street door opened. Peter dashed in.

"Thank goodness, you're here!" I exclaimed. "Where on earth have you been? Stella is terribly upset."

"I've been trying to keep you out of trouble."

"What do you mean?"

"When I woke up I decided to have some ice-water. I realized that the key to that apartment had been taken from the tray. I figured you had started off on a detective spree. The doorman told me you had come here. I saw Martinique, who told me that you were gambling. Then Enrico said you had left. I tried to find you. I called the hotel to see if you had returned."

"Well, I'm glad you're here. Find Stella and Henrietta."

"Mrs. Wayne? What is she doing here?" he exclaimed.

"Martinique wants to marry Stella; he is trying to use Henrietta as a club. He evidently knows she would hate a scandal."

"Marry Stella! Why, the dirty . . ." He started away.

"Peter, wait! There's nothing to worry about! I . . ."

"The hell there isn't!" he shouted back at me. "I'll show him!"

He was gone, and once more I was alone.

I don't know how long I waited. I did then the thing which had annoyed me with Henrietta. I left the gallery and went back to the foyer. It was still deserted. The door to Martinique's office was open. I stepped inside. It, too, was empty. I felt a sense of frustration and rage. Had he gone? Had my threat meant nothing to him?

I'd show him. I'd call the police from his office, on his own telephone. I closed the door to the beer and passed behind the desk to get to the telephone. I hesitated a moment. It was a wild and improbable story I had to tell the police.

As I stood there trying to formulate some plausible coherent story. I remembered the bracelet I had seen on my first visit. Automatically I opened the drawer. The bracelet was still there. I lifted I out and looked at it. It fascinated me. Why I did what I did I do not know. I have never stolen anything, even a man's affection, but I dropped that bracelet into my pocket unthinkly. At least I was aware of no thought process. I haven't been able to analyze it since but that action of mine has made me a little more tolerant of others. It must have been a temptation that I did not want to resist. I probably cared more about those old family heirlooms than I had realized. At any rate it went into the pocket of my skirt as a slight sound made me turn round guiltily. I was afraid Martinique had caught me in the act. At that moment a full consciousness of my guilt struck home. I was trapped.

I was relieved to find the room still empty. I could not understand it. Definitely there had been a noise quite as if the panel to the lift had opened. I turned.

"Not so fast," a high falsetto voice warned. I was startled. There was no one in the room and yet that voice seemed right in my ear. For a moment I thought it was the talk-a-phone box on the desk.

"Stay where you are," the voice commanded. "I want that bracelet." Then the panel of the lift opened a little and a woman's arm appeared. The hand was holding a gun—that was terrifying enough but even more startling was the gold band just above the wrist. It was a duplicate of the bracelet, the mate to the one in my pocket.

"Hang the bracelet over the barrel of the gun," the voice commanded. "Hurry!"

What to do? She was so determined to get it. She had a gun. Where were the others? Why didn't they come?

"Hurry!" she warned. "Step forward!"

I backed away. I don't know why but keeping the bracelet suddenly seemed very important.

"If you move another inch, I'll shoot," she warned.

It was quite likely that she would. There was one chance and I took it. The woman obviously did not want to be seen. Heedless of the warning, expecting the shot at any moment, I backed away.

I felt like a rabbit held by the gaze of a snake. The bore of the gun fascinated me. Death might hurtle from it at any moment. I didn't want to die like that. I didn't want to die at all. To face any person with a leveled gun takes more than a little courage but to back away from an unknown, unseen adversary tears at the moral fiber. I was quivering, my legs were weakening. Could I get to the door before she fired?

"Fool!" she hissed.

I expected the shot then. I hastened my backward stride. At last I was at the door. I reached back still watching that dark round hole. I tugged as the knob. The door opened as if some one was pushing it toward me. The weight of it shoved me forward. I wanted to slide round the edge of the door to safety. I saw the gun barrel waver. This is it, I thought, and steeled myself. The next minute something came out of the door and landed at my feet with a thud.

I have never had any sympathy for a screaming woman. Yet I wanted to scream but the sound died in my throat. At my feet lay Martinique, dead as he was ever going to be. It was unbelievable! He couldn't be dead! But he was. There would be no question about that glaze over his eyes. I couldn't move for a minute, just stood there looking down. When I did move the arm with the gun had gone, the panel was closed. I was alone with that awful man.

I did not want to be found there with him There would be too much explaining to do. I wanted to get away. I looked about the room stunned. In my terror at facing that gun I had backed across the room instead of sideways towards the exit into the hall. The door I had opened was to the closet at the end of the recess. Shocked as I was and knowing the danger I ran I had sense enough to wipe the knob of the closet door. I left it open. I then crossed to the door leading to the hall and wiped that knob free of prints. Thoughts tumbled through my mind. Peter and Stella would be suspected. Especially Peter because of that quarrel in the hotel lobby. If we were lucky we might get clear of the whole awful mess;

there were so many others that perhaps we might escape. Under more normal circumstances I would have sounded the alarm at once but I didn't think it wise then because there was nothing normal about it. I had threatened him. Miss Alvera had heard me. Well, if she remembered that, it might keep the children out of it. While I felt quite confident that none of us were in any way connected with his death I knew, nevertheless, that our reasons for being there would eventually be investigated. There would be endless questions to be avoided if possible. With my handkerchief under my hand I turned the knob of the foyer door and stepped out. Fortunately the foyer was empty. In the gallery I heard Henrietta ask petulantly, "Now here is she, Peter?"

I hurried to them. Stella was with them. I grasped Peter's arm. "Take them away from here!" I said, trying to keep my teeth from chattering.

"What has happened?" he asked as I hurried toward the door.

"Take Stella to the hotel and wait there until I come. Get away from here and stay away! Don't questions now."

I watched them go with relief and turned back into the gallery.

CHAPTER FOUR

THE GALLERY WAS deserted now. The foyer too was empty and the door of Martinique's office was tightly closed just as I had left it. I hurried past that grim door and ran down the stairs. If Enrico was surprised to see me he gave me no sign as I asked him to let me out through the apartment building.

He nodded.

"I'm tired and want to get away from my friends," I explained.

He said no word as he opened the door for me.

I hurried along a dimly lighted corridor. There was so little time. I wanted to see the Dast apartment before Martinique's body was discovered, to confirm my opinions if possible and get back to the hotel with the others. The long corridor ended at a fire door which opened into the second-floor hail of an apartment building.

I looked at the key. The number three-twelve was stamped on its head. On the third floor I paused for a moment to make certain that I was alone in the corridor. I didn't want to be seen. I hesitated before the door and listened. There was no sound.

Quickly I inserted the key and stepped into a small, dimly lighted hall. I waited again but there was no sound. I fumbled for a light switch. A dull orange bulb revealed three doors. The one directly in front of me opened into a small kitchen. At my right I could see the outline of a bed. The other door had to lead to the living-room. I made a quick survey of the apartment and returned at once to the living-room. The place had a rather dank, musty smell and needed a good old-fashioned airing.

It was as silent as a tomb. The living-room had not been touched since the fracas. A tile-topped coffee table lay overturned on the floor. That was the only evidence of a struggle except for the highball glasses that had rolled across the floor after their fall. There were a number of half-empty glasses dotted about the room, giving out the stale odor of not too good liquor.

I tried to re-enact the fight as they had related it to me. Their description had been vivid. I rather fancied I knew the exact spot where the man Harold had fallen. I bent down and went over the floor for bloodstains. There were none, or rather there was nothing there that seemed to be blood. I would have given anything at that moment for a Sherlock Holmes magnifying-glass and a tube of that amazing liquid that Inspector Conklin carried in his little satchel. I have seen him darken a room, sprinkle some of his liquid about and each time I have waited breathlessly for the blue glow that always appears when there is any blood.

Peter and Stella both stated that Harold's shirt front had been bloodstained. Why then was there no trace of anything that looked like blood? Martinique for all his care had not had the room cleaned. That was strange, very strange.

I sat down for a moment and tried to think what must have happened. My eye chanced on a Christmas cactus which hung limply over the edge of its pot. All the life had gone out of it. Lack of water, I thought, and leaned forward to press my finger into the earth in which it had been planted. The dirt was moist, quite soggy. That was strange, because I know that all members of the cactus family can live for long periods without water, yet this plant was dying in saturated earth.

As I flicked the wet grains of dirt from my fingers my suspicions were instantly aroused. That dirt had a peculiar odor. The next moment I was on my knees sniffing at the pot. It reeked of gin. If Peter and Stella were both intoxicated, as they so freely admitted, who then had poured gin into the flower-pot? The answer was obvious. Harold Dast was not as drunk as he had pretended to be, probably was not drunk at all. Why? Had he planned to get Peter under the influence of liquor so that he would not know what was happening? Had Dast then hoped that Stella, also intoxicated, would make an easy and willing companion for the night? I dismissed that idea. It was too simple. There had to be something more than that.

Stella had said that the boys were on their feet struggling for the gun when the shot was fired. I wanted to find the bullet if it were still in the room. Of course I knew if it had remained in the body my task was hopeless. I decided to look anyhow. I went over the wall surfaces, then along the baseboards. There was no trace of plaster on the floor and no rips in the woodwork. I went over the double door which concealed the in-a-door-bed but found nothing. I had given up all hope of finding anything when I saw a tiny wad on the floor just under the edge of the couch. I took that innocent-looking little wad and wrapped it in my handkerchief.

I didn't want anyone to know I had been in the room. I knew I had to be careful. Knowing how incriminating fingerprints can be, I was busy going over the surfaces of the things I had touched, wiping away any possible trace of myself, even the floor and the baseboards where I had knelt—when a slight sound startled me. It came from the hall. To say my blood froze in my veins for a moment is a trite phrase but that is literally what happened.

There I was on the floor like any charwoman going about her business. I felt my heart thumping soundly as I looked up, startled. The one thing I did not want was to be found in that apartment. I tried to tell myself as I raised my eyes that the sound I had heard was something outside the apartment, in the corridor perhaps, but I knew I was wrong because as my eyes left the floor I saw a pair of stylishly clad feet pointed in my direction. The mind plays curious tricks with us. Why should I think of open-front shoes and carmined toe-nails with repugnance as I knelt there on the floor and let my eyes run upward from those shoes over sheer silk stockings to a short skirt barely below the knee and on upward to the startled face under a tea-strainer hat.

It was Alice French, the girl from the plane. Even then her lacerated fingers were at her lips. Her eyes were wide with amazement. I was as much of a shock to her as she was to me, perhaps more. As I slowly rose to my feet she said, "Well!"—nothing else—and then repeated the word as if the repetition would in some strange way explain my being there at all.

In a long life of varied experiences I have found that it puts the other person on the defensive and to great disadvantage if he is made to speak first. I looked at her, using my near-sighted squint, and waited for her to speak.

She had to give in. She felt the necessity of saying something. So many people do, you know. She could have swung on her heel and walked out, leaving me to wonder what she was doing there and why, but she didn't. Very few people can resist the temptation to talk, no matter what the circumstances.

"What are you doing here?" she asked nervously. "How did you get in?"

"With a key," I replied brazenly, for the truth was as good as anything.

"You got a nerve," she accused. "How'd you get the key? Was it out—?" She didn't finish the question, just stared at me.

"H'm?" I answered vaguely as if I hadn't quite heard her.

"You heard me, Grandma," she replied contemptuously. I don't know why but I hate being called Grandma by well-meaning people, and when other people use the word with an unmistakable inflection my dander rises.

"Don't call me Grandma!" I snapped back.

"Why are you here?" she demanded.

I decided to be bold and risk a shot in the dark. "I'm a friend of Harold's," I said.

"When did you see him?" she asked cautiously.

"I haven't yet. What right have you to question me"

"The right of any woman who lives with and loves a man. How did you get in here?"

"With a key," I repeated.

"But how did you know where to find the key?"

"That was arranged by telegram," I replied.

"He made a date with you here?" She couldn't quite believe that. "Is that why you were on the plane? No, you came to . . ."

I interrupted her with, "I knew him in New York when he was in the theater there. We are old friends."

"I'll say you're old," she said mercilessly. "You ought to be ashamed of yourself, a woman of your age running after a young boy."

So that was what she thought of me! I felt relieved. I'd been accused of that before simply because I happen to like young people, always have and always will. My interest in youth is one of the things that has helped to keep me young in spirit and in mind. I had to answer her, however, and did. "What right have you to question me, since we are both in a man's apartment?" I demanded.

"It's my apartment too, if you must know. I live here with him. Does that mean anything to you?"

"Your apartment! Why yes, of course. I thought . . ."

"Never mind what you thought. I live here."

"But you registered at the hotel. I saw you."

"Perhaps I didn't want him to know I was in town for reasons of my own, reasons like this," she added angrily.

"Then he used to live here with you?" I asked.

"Why did you say that?" she asked quickly.

"Say what?"

"You spoke as if he didn't live here any more. Why did you say it like that?" There were tears in her eyes, terror in her voice.

"No reason."

"Did he send you?"

"I told you that Harold . . ."

"I know that but what I want is the truth. Did Martinique send you?"

"Martinique! No!"

She seemed relieved at that. "Please go away. Leave Harold alone."

"But we had a business appointment," I protested.

"And what were you doing on the floor there?"

That was a shrewd question and one that needed an immediate answer. "I dropped some pills. They are very small and very expensive. I was trying to find them."

She turned and ran down the short hall to the bedroom. I heard dresser drawers being hastily opened and shut. She was back in a moment demanding, "Was he going to sell you some jewelry?"

"I might have bought some," I replied warily, glad of the lead she had given me.

"Well, take a tip from me and don't. It's hot stuff. Don't buy it unless you want to get into trouble. The fool!" She whipped the words out with bitter vehemence and at the moment all her anger was for Harold. She went on as if she were thinking aloud. "Some day he's gonna get himself in trouble working old dames like you with that stuff. Now, you don't look like the type that would take a fleecing sitting down. I watched you on the plane. You weren't born yesterday. You've been around. You wouldn't just take it."

"I wouldn't," I assured her; "and thanks for the tip."

"I knew I had to come here." She started biting at the torn fragments of her nails as if she weren't quite sure until I wanted to say, "Stop it!" but I didn't.

"I always play my hunches," I said.

"So do I." Her eyes gave me a thorough going-over before she went on. "I'm going to play one now. Take my advice and get out of here or you'll be sorry."

I was ready to go but didn't feel that I should give in to her too easily. "Without seeing him?" I asked.

"Forget that you ever saw him. Go back to your hotel and, better yet, go back to New York. Some day you'll be glad of the advice. Look at this place. You can tell the sort of thing that has been going on here while I've been away." Her hands swept the room. It looked much more innocent than it really was but she, poor thing, didn't know what I knew. "You look respectable. You wouldn't want to be mixed up in anything sordid, would you?" she asked.

"No. I wouldn't."

"Then go away." She pointed to the door as if that would end it. She stepped forward and gathered up several of the highball glasses and stacked them one inside the other.

"Is that one of the hot pieces?" I asked as I indicated a lovely old gold necklace, a perfect match to the bracelet.

"No. Go away, will you?"

I started for the door. She stopped me. "I'll tell him you were here. What's your name?"

"Thomas," I said without thinking, "Ethel Thomas."

"Thomas," she repeated. "I know you now. You're the detective dame. That's why you were with them, that's why you are here. Pills, eh! And I fell for it! What were you looking for there on the floor?"

"Pills," I repeated.

She moved over and barred my exit. For a moment I was afraid I would have to fight my way out, so determined was the look in her eyes. But I was wrong.

"Look," she begged. "Give us a chance. Harold and me. We are going away. Honest! I don't know who hired you but couldn't you say that you found nothing? Please give us a chance to get out of this. We're desperate."

"I haven't been hired by anybody. I'm not really a detective. Crime has been a hobby with me. You have nothing to fear. I'll never tell the police."

"Then why are you here?"

"I've told you."

"And I don't believe you. I saw you with Peter Bradley. Why do you have to stick your nose in other people's business, making trouble for them, making them miserable?"

"I've never done that. I've tried to help people who have been in trouble."

She looked at me carefully, weighing, considering. I realized that I was being tried in her scales and suddenly I wanted to be found worthy. There was something beyond the fear in her eyes that intrigued me, something that made me pity her. It was a bruised quality. The girl had suffered in the past and would suffer in the future. I wanted, if I could, to spare her some future suffering. I would have spoken but a wave of her arm stopped me.

"Are you on the level?" she asked.

"I am."

"And did you mean what you said about helping people out of difficulties?"

"Yes."

"Would you help us?"

"That would depend."

"We haven't done anything very wrong yet. That's why we want to get out while we can. Things are crowding in on us and we don't like it. I couldn't pay you very much, because I haven't much. I've been trying to make a comeback in pictures and I made a mistake that has caught up with me. The price isn't worth the work I'll have to do. I guess no matter how rotten a person is there is one decent thing that he will hold on to. I'm like that. I don't know what to do, where to turn. I thought he'd be here and he isn't. I'm afraid. Have you seen him today?" she asked anxiously.

"No. I haven't."

"I don't know what to do. He was supposed to come to the hotel but he didn't. He isn't dead, is he? If he is, tell me," she begged. "I can stand the truth better than fear, worry and dread."

"I don't believe he is dead," I tried to reassure her. "Why should he be dead? He wasn't ill, was he?"

"No. Look! I can get money, a lot of money."

"I don't want money, child."

"Oh, if you would help us!"

"That would depend of course on your trouble," I replied.

"Did you ever get sucked into something that you hated but something so powerful that you couldn't get away?" she asked.

Her eyes were soft and gentle but still hurt as she looked at me. She was a pathetic creature sanding there. "No, I never have," I replied honestly. "I've been in some tight places but I don't think that is quite what you mean."

She shook her head. "No. That isn't what I mean. I shouldn't have asked. I can tell by looking at you that you wouldn't. You're strong. You don't get into our kind of trouble."

"If telling me will help you, go ahead. I'm not afraid, but be sure you want to confide in me. I've been the recipient of confidences before and I have found that more times than not the person who confided in me regretted it afterward. Be sure you won't be like that."

"Sometimes a person reaches a point when they have to talk," she said, "even though they are sorry for it afterward. I'm like that now. I was out here a few years ago and doing all right, but I went loco the way so many people do. I guess having a lot of money when you ain't used to it is the thing that does it. Anyhow it makes you feel cocky and well-satisfied with yourself. You have money and money is power because it protects you, gives you clothes, comforts and a sense of independence. I lost all that and the going has been tough. I wanted to come back, to regain some of that feeling of independence and assurance that I lost. I thought I knew what I was doing but I didn't. I picked the wrong way again because I fell for the influence stuff. I've had a few parts but what has it brought me? Nothing. No," she corrected herself, "I won't say that. I met Harold. That made living in a dump like this worthwhile until pressure was brought to bear on me and I found that the influence I sought was demanding a heavy price for the parts I wanted in pictures." She paused, uncertain whether to go on or not. Her fingers went to her lips.

Poor child. My heart ached for her. I knew instinctively that her problem was in some way connected with Peter and Stella and I was anxious to have her go on. I knew I was about to get some valuable information.

"Look, if I tell you all of it, if you agree to help us you will be putting yourself on the spot. You will be in the same kind of a jam that we are because I put you in it. There has been no escape for us so far and maybe there will be none for you. I'm warning you. We may drag you down with us." She moved to the window and looked out onto the street. I had moved back into the room away from the door into the hall and was standing near the bed closet.

"I've always been able to take care of myself. I'm not afraid," I assured her. I waited for an answer, I don't know how long. The doorbell rang.

When she turned she was opposite the door leading into the hall. I expected her to speak, but her lips clamped shut in a tight line as her eyes filled with a new terror. As I was about to speak she moved toward me and put a warning finger to her lips. She came quickly to my side, opened the bed closet and thrust me in, giving me no time to think, no chance to question the wisdom of the move.

Normally I do not allow myself to be pushed about but this time I could not battle the fear and desperation so evident in her eyes and movement. As the door moved shut I thought I heard her give a sigh of relief.

The place was dark and stuffy, full of the faint taint of human flesh that is left on soiled linen and bedclothes not changed often enough. I felt a little sick, but more than that I was afraid. A chill ran up my spine and settled uncomfortably at the base of my skull. The girl was an actress. Had I allowed myself to be thrust into a trap? Had she out-generaled me? Was I to die in that closet? I took a deep breath. I have never had claustrophobia but I wasn't sure that I didn't have a touch of it right then. I took a second breath while my heart pounded. Mentally I tried to ignore the stale smell, discarding it for the fresher air that I knew came in under the crack of the door. No matter what happened to me I was not to die of suffocation.

CHAPTER FIVE

WHAT WAS GOING to happen to me? Had she thrust me into the closet to protect herself so that I might help her in the future? Of what was she afraid? Would she leave me in that closet until Martinique's body had been discovered? What was she doing? She had talked as if she had expected to find Harold at the apartment. Where was he?

He was the one link in the chain I knew I could forge to our benefit, for there was no doubt about her love for Harold Dast. From what I had heard from the children I had not thought much of Harold as a person. You know how your mind runs ahead of a story, how you form opinions of people you have never met. There had to be something good in Harold to breed the love she so obviously felt. Time would tell. I was getting as philosophical as was possible in the narrow confines of that cell with the spectre of a bed beside me. In the dim gray-black light I could see the wires of the coiled springs like rows of snakes ready to spring at me. Why does the human mind run to horrible things? Why can't we think of peace and beauty as automatically as we think of unpleasant things? Why is our natural inclination to think the worst first?

I wish there was some means of measuring thought. So much can flit through a person's mind in so short a time, so many memories and impressions, hates, hopes and fears can tumble one upon the other in a fraction of time which measured in thought becomes an eternity. I was marshaling my wits, trying to prepare myself for what might come, when Alice's voice demanded angrily, "What are you doing here?"

There was a deep silence.

"Answer me," she insisted.

"You know. Why do you ask me? You know everything. Cut the comedy," a familiar voice replied brazenly.

"Have you seen him?"

"No."

"Then why are you here?" There was desperation in Alice's voice.

"Any reason why I shouldn't see Harold?" I recognized that familiar voice then. It was Auriel Dodd.

"Plenty," Alice said defiantly. I could hear her move, could imagine the revolt that must be appearing in those terror-laden eyes. I'd like to have seen her then asserting herself as she tossed defiance, fighting to keep her hold on the man she loved.

"So, you're afraid you can't hold him," Auriel taunted.

"I can hold him all right, if we are left alone," Alice replied with vehemence.

"He's been on the market for some time, anybody's man, so to speak, hasn't he?"

"You're just saying that. I know all about you. He told me," Alice said defiantly. "Did Martinique send you back here?"

"No. Why should he?"

"I don't know." Alice's reply was tortured. Poor child, she seemed to feel that the world was against her and Harold.

"Where is Harold?" Auriel asked.

"I don't know."

"If you're expecting him here I'll wait. I'd really like to see him," Auriel suggested.

Good heavens! How long was I to be cooped up in that closet. I was about to step out but changed my mind.

"I'm not expecting him; I just thought he might be here," Alice replied. "Stay if you like. I'm going."

"I might wait a few minutes. After all, I have an appointment," Auriel said. "Have a cigarette."

"No. Goodbye."

I heard Alice's sharp heels thump into the hall. As I strained my ears I thought I heard a door close. Had she gone and left me stranded? I certainly, on second thought, did not want Auriel Dodd to know that I was in that closet.

Auriel Dodd was moving about the room. She had given a low laugh at Alice's exit. I thought I heard a match strike but I was not sure. A moment later I did hear something strike against an ash-tray, then a chair creaked.

I was wondering if she had told the truth. Perhaps she did have an appointment. If so then my convictions were correct. Harold Dast was not dead. Then what game was he playing of his own, pitting those two women, one against the other?

Auriel must have turned in her chair at some noise which I could not hear, for she definitely moved. A moment later I heard steps in the little hall of the apartment, thought I felt the vibration of those steps within the closet. Auriel must have stood up just then.

"I was just about to go," she said. "Alice French was here." She laughed. "She's gone. Went away in a huff. What is the matter?"

Whoever it was who had come into the room was moving about.

"She's gone, I tell you," Auriel insisted with a trace of nervousness in her voice. "There's no one here but me. She thought I had come to see him—as if I would! Why did you want to see me? What have you to tell me?"

Auriel Dodd was afraid of the person in the room with her. Why? What was going on? Why didn't the person speak?

"I have an appointment, I'm late now. What did you want?" She seemed to be fighting against time, trying desperately to get away from the unknown person. I heard her move, then stop, then move again. Her voice had grown louder. She was very close to the door behind which I hid.

Time passed.

"No, no!" she cried in terror. I knew that she was not acting, that her terror was real. The scene going on outside that door was not a role she was assuming. She was not dramatizing the situation. I heard movement, slow movement as if she were trying to escape him. I felt the door in front of me press in as if she had backed into it, cornered, held at bay. The door closed, the lock snapped. I was locked in, a prisoner. Through that thin partition I felt a mortal terror that I believe came from her to me.

"Don't!" she screamed, but the hysteria of her cry was drowned in the short sharp snap of a shot. For one fleeting instant I hoped that she had killed him, but it was a vain hope. There was a tearing of wood, a breathless fraction of time when I thought that I too had been hit. The bullet passed very close to me and buried itself in the wall just beyond my head. As it dug into the wall it scattered a fine mist of powdered plaster in my face. I heard a few larger grains drop, their slight contact with the floor sounding like thunder in my ears. Beyond the door there was a hysterical sob, a moan, surprised, agonized, final. The pressure on the door was released, a moment of silence and then a thump just beyond me. A crumpled body sagged to the floor. I looked down. The thin edge of light was gone. I was in almost total darkness.

Through the terrible darkness and the deadly silence, I heard a voice whisper, "It had to be. This is what happens when people think they are stronger than me. They die. See?"

I had been an ear-witness to a murder. I knew the poor girl was dead. What was going to happen to me? The law of self-preservation is strong, there is no denying that. Even though I was horrified, incensed at what had happened to her I was thinking about myself. Had her body cut off my air supply? Would I be suffocated before I would dare open that door? How much longer would that horrible voice gloat over the thing that had been done? I'd make him pay for his crime! It was more than just a cold murder that enraged me. That horrible man played with human life as a cat worries a mouse. What terrible thing would be next? How would this new crime affect the children? What was I going to do? How could I combat such a creature? Would Alice French come back? If she came now, would she die too? I prayed she would not return.

I felt a little sick, but denied myself that emotional luxury. I must be quiet. He must not suspect that I was in the closet. I waited, not daring to breathe, when my every impulse was to struggle out and tear him limb from limb if I could. Reason told me there was nothing I could do then. I must wait but I did want to see his face, to be able to recognize him so that I could deal with him later. Cold calculating reason held me there uncomfortable by the self-imposed constriction of my breathing. The man was a ruthless fiend. I knew he had killed Martinique, had killed Auriel because she knew something about Martinique's death. What? Would I be able to pick up that lost clew? He would kill me as quickly and as easily as he had killed her. He must think that his crime was unknown. I must wait, no matter how long, until the road was clear. I felt my ears throb as I strained every faculty to detect the slightest sound beyond that horrible door.

I have been associated with violent death many times in the past few years, have been close to it myself because of my activities in connection with solving crimes, but this was my first experience so close to murder. At other times the deed had been done prior to my arrival on the scene; but there, separated by a few feet of space and a door, murder had been done. A new surge of revulsion wept over me. I felt terribly ill. I remembered a pet of mine that had been killed by a carriage when I was a little girl. I felt just like that. I shivered and shook until I feared my flesh would tear itself away from my bones. I was filled with a great surge of retching which I forced myself to control unless I wanted to die, quickly, secretly as she had died.

I have boasted that I am not afraid, but I knew how vain my boastings had been. Death waited for me beyond that door and I was afraid to meet it. I did not want to die. I do not know that I will ever want to die but when death comes to me in the normal course of events I hope I can meet it bravely and not be the cowering creature I was behind that door. Suddenly I knew I could not die, would not die, until that man was brought to justice.

I waited, listening, every nerve tense. There was a movement beyond the door. A new terror seized me. Suppose he opened the door thinking to hide the body in the closet. I gripped my hands until my nails dug deep into my palms. I couldn't stand that. I tried to will him away from the closet.

The next moment I heard a grunt. Just an ordinary commonplace grunt, the kind a man gives when he bends over to lift something. It was so ordinary, so much a part of everyday living that I very nearly laughed. What was he doing? I waited. I heard a piece of furniture kicked out of the way. There was a tinkle of breaking glass.

Then measured, weighted footsteps growing dimmer. I knew the sound for what it was. He was carrying the body away. I had heard that sound once before when a murderer thinking he had the body of his victim had lifted me and with that same heavy methodical tread had carried me to a fate I could not foresee. The steps grew dimmer and dimmer until there was nothing left but the thump, thump, thump of my heart, which seemed to carry on and repeat the rhythm of his going.

Even then I dared not move. I waited five, ten, fifteen terror-filled minutes. I waited in the vain hope that Alice French would return. But the room beyond was deadly silent. I have no means of knowing how long. All I knew was that I could not endure that prison any longer. I had to get out or scream.

I pressed against the door, but it would not budge.

I was locked in that dreadful closet!

My previous fear was as nothing compared to that moment of realizing that I was a prisoner in the closet. With trembling fingers I fumbled over the surface of the doors where they joined. There was no catch to release, nothing, just the bare wooden surface of the two doors where they met. I don't know yet what providence kept me from shouting and banging on those doors, unless it was a fear greater than my panic. It must have been my logical mind working, holding in check my animal instincts. An animal would have made a terrific din to bring aid. Aid was not what I wanted; I must have safety and my wily mind knew that and reasoned with me subconsciously. I knew I did not want to bring that man back. I didn't want to bring anyone into that room until I had managed my escape, not even Alice. There had to be a way out. I must control myself and think. I tried to be calm but I was like the boy who whistles in the dark.

Once again reason helped me. I drove my mind back into the past. I forced myself to think of doors, double doors, for it was a double door that held me prisoner. How did they operate, how were they locked? I knew that this one had a blind lock that operated from the outside. That gave me the clew to my difficulty. It had to be right. My hands had stopped their trembling. They were eager now as I explored the hard cold surface of the door joints looking for the way of escape that I knew must be there.

Movement in the dark, in that confined space was difficult. I was hemmed in between the edge of the bed which stood vertically between the door and the wall. The bed itself with its front legs dangling down, its springs bulging from the weight of mattress and bedding, barely cleared the door. There was but little room for my frantic fingers. I was glad I was thin. A fat arm could not have managed.

For one dreadful moment I feared my arms would not be long enough, but my sanity was coming back, holding in check my mounting terror. I squatted down as best I

could in the narrow space and with my face pressed
against the edge of the mattress I sent my arm out
serpent-like toward the lower joining of the doors. I
breathed with relief. It was there as I knew it must be, a
bolt which kept the second half of the door in place, a bolt
which was put inside the closet rather than outside
because it would have been unsightly on the front
surface. It pulled up more easily than I had hoped.
Gratified, I struggled back to my feet.

I pressed on the door but it would not open although it
was a trifle looser than it had been before. There was a
catch at the top of the door which had to be released. I
reached for the top bolt but I couldn't quite make it. I
inserted my foot on a cross-piece of the spring and pulled
myself up the several inches from the floor and with a
final straining effort I managed to free the bolt. My next
problem, I knew, was to exert enough pressure against
the doors to force the catch which held them closed. With
the proper amount of pressure they, being free at top and
bottom, would swing open. But how to exert the pressure?
I couldn't get between the bed and the door.

After a moment's deliberation I decided to pull at the
upper part of the bed, which would be the foot when it
was ready for use. I reached up and tugged. I hung by my
arms and felt the bed move toward the door. I pulled and
pulled, swung my weight off my feet. I was successful.
The weight of the bed with me pulling on it did the trick.
The doors flew open and down went the bed, making the
most ungodly racket as it thumped to the floor. The bed
was down and so was I.

I was on the floor under it unhurt, for the divine
Providence that watches over fools was with me. As the
foot of the bed crashed down to settle on its steel legs it
missed me by inches or this story would have ended right
then. I wasted no time in crawling from under that
contraption of the devil. I was on my feet in an instant. I
took one quick look about the room which had witnessed
the tragedy and prepared to leave.

The din of the falling bed was still in my ears as I cautiously peered around the door into the hall and the bedroom at the end of the apartment. There seemed to be no sound. I was afraid, however, that the tenants in the apartment below might wonder what had caused the crash and come up to investigate. I opened the door into the corridor. I heard voices below me. I didn't bother to listen to what they were saying. I darted across the corridor and crept up the stairs as quietly as I could. I didn't want to be seen anywhere near that apartment until I had had time to think. I didn't want to think or anything else until I had successfully left the building behind me. More than anything in the world I wanted some fresh air.

CHAPTER SIX

I WAS HEADED THE wrong way for escape but I did want to get away from the voices on the stairs below me. In my haste, in that crawling position, I stepped on the edge of my skirt. I pitched forward, my nose smacked against a step. I felt unaccountably dizzy. I reached out to keep myself from slipping but the steps were made of some marble-like composition; my fingers would not hold, I started going down. I had sense enough to roll over and take the steps in the bumping fashion I had enjoyed as a child. Those stairs in our old house, however, were thickly carpeted and less cruel to the anatomy. With feet out, skirts billowing over my face and sore nose I made a perfect blind five-point landing on the third floor.

The din of voices had increased but over them I heard a decided "Ouch!" as my foot struck something. When I had pulled my skirts down I looked up into the blank face of Enrico, who was bending forward to nurse a sore shin-bone.

"I must have run into you," I said stupidly.

"You did," he agreed, not too graciously, as he rubbed his shin.

Had the situation been reversed I know I should have been laughing at him. The absence of dignity, the utter lack of control when a person falls, always causes me to laugh. As it was I began to giggle as I struggled to my feet. The vision of my downward flight, skirts billowing, old-fashioned drawers showing, must have been something that the man had never seen and would probably never we again, except perhaps in a picture. As the vision took form I started to laugh. Of course, it was hysteria. I laughed so hard that I lost my balance and fell toward Enrico. He reached out an arm and caught me, holding me tightly against him for a moment until the hysteria had passed.

A group of wide-eyed people were surrounding us. As my laughter died a flood of questions poured over our heads.

"What happened?" a frizzled blonde asked.

"Was it an earthquake?" a second voice demanded.

"The lady had a fall," Enrico explained.

"We don't mean that, Enrico," the blonde said sharply. "It was something in that apartment. A terrible thud. It sounded as if the house was coming down."

"We'll see," he said.

"There's more things going on in this place," the blonde complained, and the others agreed with her. "You ought to put a stop to it."

"I'll see," Enrico said and rapped on the door of Harold's apartment.

"It's open," the blonde said sharply as the door moved under his touch.

"So it is," he agreed, and entered.

They followed him into the apartment, which gave me the moment I needed. Enrico had started me out of the gambling room ages before. I didn't want to answer his questions if he felt inclined to ask them. I took the lift to the ground floor and escaped from the building.

I should have cried, Help! Police! Murder! right then, but I did not. I had one idea and one only, to get away from that horrible sinister building and everything connected with it.

Martinique lay dead in his office. I did not stop to think then that the discovery of his body might take place at any moment, perhaps had been found and the alarm sent out. I had lost all sense of time. I had no idea how long I had been in that apartment. A woman had been killed there. Alice French had escaped death by moments. Once on the pavement I looked about half expecting to see her hidden behind some tree. The street was deserted, only the twittering of lazy birds reminded me that I was in a normal world again.

Who was the killer? I knew I could never forget the hysterical terror of the poor soul; even as I scurried along the street I could hear it ringing in my ears. I raced on. It never occurred to me to look for a cab, to even think of one. I must get away, back to the hotel. I must find Alice French.

At an intersection that would take me to Sunset Boulevard I glanced back along the way I had come. It was a peaceful street bathed in the late afternoon sun, shaded by palms, peppers and eucalyptus trees. Leaving its quiet calm I started the climb back to Sunset.

The steep grade slowed my progress. Just what was I to do? I was in a fine predicament myself. I had been an ear-witness to a murder. A girl had been killed within a few inches of me. I might have died myself had the course of the bullet been a few inches lower or had the murderer suspected that I stood flattened within that awful closet.

My breath was completely gone when I reached the Boulevard and leaned against a pole to rest. I embraced that pole as if it were a long-lost friend. It gave me reassurance. Then I remembered my clothes and began adjusting my garments. I was hot, felt sticky, my bodice was damp, spotted. The right sleeve, where I had been leaning against the pole, was stained. I was more interested in a drugstore across the street. I wove drunkenly through the racing traffic, curses at my foolhardiness ringing in my ears as annoyed drivers glowered at me.

In the haven of a telephone booth I called the hotel and asked for Alice French. I waited anxiously until the cold impersonal voice of the operator told me that she did not answer. I left a message. Alice French was to go to my room and wait there until I returned. "It is of the utmost importance," I warned the operator. "Please see that she gets it."

I felt better and went outside. Accustomed to the ways of New York I expected to hail a cruising cab. Gratefully I sank down on a bench provided for waiting bus passengers. The traffic hummed and buzzed with hypnotic regularity. My eyes, tired of the swift flight of cars, sought the relief of a longer view. In front of me lay a great section of the city spread out like an oriental carpet. For a moment I thought of this modern Bagdad, of the hopes and dreams of thousands of men, women and children seeking fame and fortune in the fabulous city, of Auriel Dodd so sure of herself that morning, of the press pictures Enrico had taken there at the airport.

Auriel Dodd—dead, cold and stiff. Where had the man taken her?

Cornered like a rat she had been shot down because she must have known the murderer of Martinique. She had to be avenged. I did not care about Martinique; I was, I think, glad that he had died.

I, who boast that I never tire, within reason, was worn out. On that bench I had my first taste of the effects of a semi-tropical climate. Normally I would have bounced off that seat and forged ahead. I didn't, however. Great weights pulled at my lids, dragging them shut. I tried to fight the overpowering desire for sleep which was en-eloping me. The next thing I knew I jerked myself awake and felt foolish sitting there on a public bench nodding in the late afternoon sun. I had slept for a few minutes, for my head had sunk forward. The quick, surprised jerk had raised Ned with my transformation, tossing it askew at what must have been a rakish angle.

I felt dazed for a moment as I blinked back to reality and tried to make myself presentable. Across the street and down the block Martinique's Gallery gleamed white and chaste, giving no hint of the horrible things that had taken place there. Vines wound up the tall columns, softening its white face. The traffic surged by. A new note jerked me to my feet. From somewhere far off I heard a police siren. At that moment a bus stopped beside me, the door jerked open and the driver asked, "Beverly Hills?"

He dropped me near the hotel. I was ready for action again.

Alice French had not returned to the hotel. A note lay in her box. Where was she? Had she returned to that apartment? I asked the church-warden clerk to see if it was my note. It was with another memorandum for her to call a number. Where was the girl?

In my room Henrietta, Stella and Peter were bored and annoyed. Henrietta's eyes chilled me as I entered the sitting-room.

"Why did you rush us away?" Stella demanded. "Nothing had been decided, nothing finished."

"It was decided for us. Martinique was murdered," I said.

Henrietta gasped. I thought she would have a heart attack. Peter and Stella were shocked at first, then seemed unable to take it in. "Who killed him?" Peter asked.

"I don't know, Peter, but with any luck I can find out." I tried to make my answer seem full of conviction but I failed miserably.

"Peter!" Stella cried. "Oh, Peter!"

I knew what she thought; so did he because he took her hand and held it with reassurance.

"Are you sure?" Henrietta finally managed to ask.

"I saw the body."

"We'll be dragged back there!" Stella cried in alarm.

"I knew it!" Henrietta complained. "I knew something terrible would happen in this awful town with these awful people."

"People are alike all over," I reminded her.

"How can you say that?" she demanded irritably. "When you know we can never face our friends again."

"Tut, tut," I said.

I don't care for prophecies of doom. As an old cook of mine always said, no matter what trouble she faced,

"What is to be will be if it never happens." That old cook was right. I knew there was no point inviting trouble. It has a way of finding one unaided. Until I could locate Alice French I felt my hands were tied.

"Some girl called you," Stella said. "She seemed frantic. She said she would call again, and did. She left no name."

I had been standing at the window looking down at the smooth velvet lawns, the palms, tulip trees, giant canna and the ever-present lantana. A figure turned up the path just as I had done a few minutes earlier. It was Alice French. "I'll be back in a moment," I promised and darted from the room to leave them utterly amazed.

I wanted to intercept that girl, to get from her the confirmation of a theory which was growing rapidly. The elevator seemed frightfully slow in coming and depositing me in the lobby. She should have reached the lobby as soon as I did. I went past the desk to the main door. She was nowhere in sight and there was no trace of her on the path coming up from the Boulevard. I ran down the steps, peered into the shrubbery.

The doorman joined me. "Lost something?" he asked solicitously.

"A friend," I replied and knew instantly how silly it sounded. I explained, "I thought I saw her coming up the path from the Boulevard."

"Haven't seen anyone in the last five minutes," he assured me as one does a child or a not quite normal person.

Alice French had vanished there in front of the hotel and no one, not even the doorman, had seen her go. Things like that just couldn't happen in a world so serenely calm and beautiful as that spot. I have heard stories of vanishing people but I had never expected to see it happen. I could raise an alarm, but the doorman was inclined to think me daft. I couldn't tell all I knew then. Anything might have happened. Why had she vanished just when she was so important to me? Disappointed, dejected, I returned to the others.

"What are we going to do?" Henrietta demanded, as if it were all my fault.

"Wait," I replied tersely. "We have some time to think out a course of action. At the moment I want a brandy and soda. How about you, Henrietta?"

"Have you any smelling-salts?" she asked in a strained voice.

"No, but I'll get you some."

"Never mind, I'll take a little brandy."

"What are we going to do?" Stella asked as I poured a drink.

"Nothing," I said. "We know nothing about Martinique's death, just remember that. If we are called back there, don't let the police trap you with their clever questioning. You know nothing, just stick to that story."

We were occupied with our own thoughts for some time after that. I had decided to say nothing about Auriel Dodd until I could find and talk with Alice French. Any statement I might make would involve the children. Who had killed Auriel? Who had killed Martinique? Why? That woman who had wanted the bracelet, was she the murderer? No, I was reasonably sure the killer had been a man.

Stella broke the silence after a long look at me. "You're a sight," she said. "You look like something out of a grab-bag. What have you been doing? Your clothes are a mess. What's that stain on your bodice?"

I had had no time to think of my appearance. I had forgotten all about the stain on my sleeve, that I had apparently picked up from that friendly pole. I was about to change, anxious to get away from that questioning look in Stella's eyes, when a loud knock sounded on the door. We all gave a guilty start. Peter jumped to his feet but I waved him back and called, "Come in."

A motorcycle officer strode in. "Miss Thomas?" he asked.

"I'm Miss Thomas."

"I'm Chitter of the West Hollywood office."

"Yes, Mr. Chitter." It had come, but I think I made a good job of bluffing it out.

"You're wanted by the police in connection with the murder of Martinique."

"Me, a murder?" I gasped.

"Yes, ma'am. And if any of these people are Peter Bradley, Stella Wayne or Mrs. Wayne we want them too."

"We are all here," I said brightly, "but I don't understand. Martinique has been murdered, you say?"

"Yes, ma'am, and I have orders to bring you in."

"But we . . ." I began a protest.

"I only know my orders," Chitter said stubbornly. "I was told to bring you in. If you want to make a fuss over it, I suppose you can."

"Fuss?" I repeated.

"I'd advise you to come along," he said, ignoring my repetition of his word.

"Of course," I agreed.

"And say," he added, "you ain't got a man by the name of Harold Dast here with you, have you?"

"I never heard of him," I said.

"Well, I was just trying. It would have been nice to get the whole load."

"'Were there others?" I asked.

"Yes, ma'am. Auriel Dodd, she's an actress, and Tim Flannigan, he's an agent."

"Everybody couldn't have killed him, could they?" I asked.

"I don't know, lady, them was the orders. Now if you're ready, I'll get a wagon." He moved toward the telephone.

"Are we under arrest?" I asked.

"No. Orders didn't say nothing about arresting you, just to bring you in for questioning."

"Then we can go in Mrs. Wayne's car. I don't like wagons," I stated flatly.

"But it ain't a wagon, lady. It's a name for a police . . ."

"I know what it is and I don't intend to ride in it unless I'm under arrest."

"But . . ."

"Now listen, Captain," I said. "You carry the riff-raff of the criminal world in those wagons. We'll take the car and you can escort us. It will be quicker and much more comfortable."

"Okay, lady. I wouldn't want to get lousy myself. Let's get going," he suggested amiably. I think he liked being called captain.

With Chitter looking very elegant and officious on his motorcycle, we roared away from the hotel.

"The fat is in the fire now," Peter remarked wryly.

"I'll try to pull it out for you if you'll just remember that you know nothing," I cautioned again. "The police will have to prove everything against us, and I rather believe they will move slowly."

"I don't like Harold Dast being brought into this. I can't understand it," Stella said.

"Why do you suppose they want him?" Peter wondered.

"I'm more interested in who killed Martinique and why?" I replied, because his death left me with a double mystery on my hands rather than the one I had anticipated.

"Whoever did it had a good reason," Peter declared.

"He deserved to die," Henrietta agreed.

"The time has come . . ." I said, as we drove up to the entrance of the Gallery with a flourish.

Chitter had pulled in ahead of the car and was occupied with the crowd which had collected about the entrance. We were all startled as the door on the street side of our car opened and a young man popped in with us.

"My name's Tweed," he said. "Reporter! I want to get inside." I had but a fleeting glimpse of his pert face and gay eyes as he grinned at us. "Don't give me away, will you?"

I made no reply. If the man was clever enough to get in I had no intention of stopping him. I'd rather have a reporter on my side than against me any time, particularly in a murder case.

CHAPTER SEVEN

AS WE LEFT THE car and hurried across the pavement some flashbulbs went off. Chitter was ahead of us busy opening a passage. Tweed trotted along in the wake of my skirts. The next moment we were all inside. The attention, of course, was directed to us. Tweed had gained his entrance. He slipped away.

Chitter was proud and well satisfied with himself as he herded us across the room. At the entrance to the foyer we were halted while Chitter went ahead to make his report.

I looked back. Tweed gave me a smile and a salute with a wave of his hand. He was young, eager and the most thoroughly alive person I had seen for some time. He was animation itself. His eyes danced as his lips parted in a quick smile. He walked on the balls of his feet and seemed about to fly at any moment. I liked him, liked his ingenuity and his saucy freckled face. His movements seemed casual but there was purpose behind them. By the time Chitter returned for us, Tweed was again at my elbow.

"Come along," Chitter said. Tweed stepped beside me. "Here, you, where do you think you are going?" Chitter demanded.

"With Miss Thomas, of course," Tweed replied. "She's a friend of mine."

Since I made no denial Chitter took us past the policeman. We were taken to Martinique's office. "Here she is, Inspector, and the others too," Clutter announced proudly.

The Inspector was standing in the middle of the room. He was a short man with sandy-blond hair, and a mustache just a shade darker. His clear blue eyes were amused as he looked at us and said, "Well, if it isn't Barnaby Tweed! Now, how did you get in?"

"He's a friend of mine, Inspector," I said.

"Is he now?" the Inspector queried. He turned to Tweed. "Do you mind telling me just how you happen to be the bosom friend of a lady who hasn't been in this town twenty-four hours?"

"I get around, Duncan," Tweed replied.

"I know you do. Sometimes your agility amazes me. See how fast you can get out."

"Have a heart, Inspector. Be reasonable for once in your life."

Inspector Duncan looked at me. "Do you want him here?"

"He has promised that he will print nothing without my approval," I replied.

"So you're the famous Ethel Thomas, amateur detective, writer of mystery stories? Tell me, Miss Thomas, how did you get mixed up in this crime?"

"Mixed isn't quite the word," I said. "I was unfortunate enough to have been here earlier this afternoon."

Tweed interrupted, "Let me telephone one line to the paper will you, Duncan? Just this: Ethel Thomas, famous author-detective on hand at killing of Martinique. That will 'wow' them."

"No!" Duncan said crisply, with emphasis that was not to be denied.

"Should I throw him out, Inspector?" Chitter asked eagerly from the doorway.

"No, he's all right. Tell Smith to bring the others in."

"Are you the Inspector Duncan?" I asked.

"I'm the only one out here," he answered. "Why?"

"Inspector Conklin of New York is a friend of mine. He told me to look you up."

"Too bad you didn't," he said crisply.

"There wasn't time," I answered.

"You're Stella Wayne, and I presume you're Peter Bradley," Duncan said, ignoring my overtures. "Is this Mrs. Wayne?"

Henrietta made a frigid acknowledgment.

The door opened. A fair, anemic, youngish man entered with book and pencil in his hand.

"Take the desk, Crawford," Duncan instructed. Tim Flannigan entered, his eyes darkly brooding. Enrico and Miss Alvera were next.

"Sit down," Duncan said.

Some of the men, Peter included, were too nervous to sit. Tweed came and sat on a bench beside me.

"Thanks, pal," he whispered.

Duncan faced us. "We are investigating a murder," he began. "A murder which took place in this room, at that desk. The victim was Martinique. He was shot in the back. The murderer did not have the courage to face his victim. You are here because in our preliminary investigation we have found that all of you were closely associated with Martinique in some way, were here this afternoon at the time of the murder. You are here now for questioning. As you know, you cannot be forced to speak; at the same time if you do talk anything that you say can be held against you." He looked us over but no one spoke. "By your silence I assume you are ready for me to go on."

"Would it do any good to object?" Flannigan asked, his voice booming through the room.

"It would delay matters. I could take you to headquarters, you could arrange to have a lawyer act for you, he could get you out on bail. I could then re-arrest you as material witnesses and hold you for several days, weeks, months perhaps while your lawyers battled with the courts. You wouldn't have to talk during that time," Duncan said with a sly smile curling the corners of his mouth.

"Not for me," Flannigan said heartily. "I'll talk"

"Anyone wish to object?" Duncan asked. There was another restless silence.

"Very well. I'll begin with you, Miss Thomas." The others settled back with a rustle of nervous relief but it was only for a moment, for Duncan said, "The rest of you will wait outside. I have a method of my own in cases like this. I'll keep Miss Thomas here. When I am through with her, I'll call the next witness. Miss Thomas will stay; each of you as you are called will remain in this room with me. While you wait I do not expect you to have any conversation whatsoever with your neighbor. Is that straight?" They nodded in silent understanding and moved toward the door.

"May I stay, Inspector?" Tweed begged.

"I wouldn't let you out of my sight now, Tweed," he replied.

"Any special orders?" a policeman at the door asked.

"Keep them separated and no conversation. Chitter, you stay here. Have you reported where you are?"

Chitter nodded. "My relief man is covering the Boulevard."

They were gone. I waited. Crawford at the desk sat with poised pencil.

"Your full name, please," Duncan said.

"Ethel Thomas. I am living at the Beverly Hotel," I answered.

Always my inclination is to side with the police, to tell them all the facts of a case. Normally I would have done so. I'd have told Inspector Conklin everything because I know him, but this shrewd man facing us—I knew nothing about him whatever. There had been a double murder—the children were caught in a net. There seemed no good reason at that moment to tell him all that I knew. Since the circumstances were very suspicious, since they had a definite motive for ridding themselves of Martinique, it seemed best to me then to keep ourselves out of the case if possible.

He smiled. "You were the last known person to be with Martinique," he stated. "Was he alive when you saw him?"

"He was," I replied. "But your information has been faulty. I was not the last person to see him alive to my knowledge."

"Meaning what, Miss Thomas?"

Crawford's pencil was racing across the paper as I replied.

"I left here two hours ago. Has he been dead all that time?"

"We don't know yet. As far as we know you were the last person to enter the room before the body was discovered."

"I wouldn't know about that."

"But you did come back to this room just before you left the building," he insisted.

"I came to the door and looked in. The room was empty. Martinique was not at his desk," I replied, wondering what he had heard, how much he knew.

"You are sure about that?"

"Positive."

"But you would have come in, had he been here?"

"Yes."

"And you didn't enter the room that last time?"

"No. My friends had just come up from the gambling rooms. We left at once," I stated.

"Then you had nothing important to say to Martinique?"

"Not then."

"And that is your story?" he asked.

"It is."

"Why did you come here at all, Miss Thomas?"

"I had heard about the place, the antiques, glass, jewelry—and the gambling," I added.

"Gambling?" he queried.

"Yes, gambling. Don't tell me you haven't heard?" I retorted.

He smiled at that.

"And, furthermore, since you are interested in all the people who were here this afternoon, people who had a grievance against Martinique or the place, where is the man who came to look for his wife and made a scene in the gambling room, where is the woman who insisted that she see Martinique because she claimed the game was crooked?"

"That's interesting. I'll look into that," he promised.

"The man, Enrico, knows all about it," I said.

"We will come to that later. You insist you had no good reason for being here. Let's say no ax to grind."

"He wasn't killed with an ax, was he?" I asked. I saw Crawford stifle a chuckle as he wrote. "You told us, Inspector, that he was shot in the back."

"I'm disappointed in you, Miss Thomas. I had hoped a woman of your experience would be helpful. As a matter of fact, I expected it. You didn't enter the room that last time?"

"No."

"Bring Enrico in," he said to Chitter who was leaning against the door. I knew then he neither believed nor trusted me.

"Your full name, please," he greeted Enrico. "Enrico Juaquin."

"Where do you live?"

"In the apartment next door."

"'What is your position here?"

"I manage the place for Martinique," Enrico replied softly.

"Who would want to murder Martinique?" Duncan demanded.

Enrico shrugged. "I could not say."

"Did he have enemies?"

"There were many people who were not too friendly but I do not think they would murder him," Enrico stated quietly.

"Why not?"

Enrico considered that for a moment. "It is hard to say in words something that you feel. Many people feared Martinique and his influence, many people hated him but they were very afraid. I say this badly. You know what I mean perhaps?"

"I suppose you mean that their fear was greater than their hate, that they would not kill him because they were afraid of the consequences," Duncan suggested.

"Yes," Enrico agreed. "The consequences."

"But someone has killed him, fear or no fear," Duncan remarked.

"I know," Enrico acknowledged. "I must have been wrong then."

"Just why did people fear him?" Duncan demanded.

"I do not know that. I only know what I could see and feel as people came and went. They handled him with kid gloves."

I knew the man was trying to fool Duncan, was holding back information just as I had held it back. Enrico knew much about Martinique's business, I was positive of that. He was being too agreeable, too bland, too smooth. He looked different too. Why? He had changed his suit, was in darker clothes.

"We want to fix the approximate time of the murder," Duncan said. "I want you to tell me what happened just before the body was found. We have had several statements but we want to get them straight now."

"I do not know when he was killed," Enrico denied quickly.

"Neither do I. That's what I'm after. There were a number of people in and out of this office this afternoon. When were you here last?"

Enrico shifted. "It must have been two hours ago. I don't remember positively."

"We think he has been dead that long," Duncan said pointedly.

Enrico threw me a quick startled look that made me very uncomfortable.

"Two hours ago," he repeated thoughtfully.

"Yes. Don't get away from the point," Duncan warned.

"I had been in the gambling rooms," Enrico said easily. "I came up for money. It's in the safe in the offices across the hail. As I came up the stairs I saw Mr. Flannigan leave Martinique's office."

"See anyone else?"

"No. Just Flannigan."

"Did you speak to Flannigan?"

"No."

"How did he act? Was he in a hurry? Would you say, thinking back on it, that he was excited?"

I found myself thinking that Duncan should not put ideas into Enrico's head.

"He acted all right," Enrico said. "He came out and slammed the door behind him."

I hoped that that statement might be useful to me if Duncan became too suspicious. I felt that Enrico was giving me a much needed alibi.

"Then there was nothing furtive about his leaving the place?"

"No. He made noise. He strode out like a man who doesn't give a damn for anything."

"How long were you in that other office?"

"A few minutes. I don't know. I opened the safe, took out some money, made an entry in the book, made a memorandum for Martinique, glanced at some papers on the desk, closed the safe. I did not hurry. It was perhaps five minutes," he ended thoughtfully.

"Did you see anyone as you left that office?"

"I saw Miss Thomas before I left."

I flashed a look at him. My hopes sank. I had not seen him nor had I seen Flannigan when he left.

"Just where was Miss Thomas?"

"She was in the main gallery in one of the small showrooms."

"Did she see you?"

"No. There are overhead mirrors in the private offices so that we can see into the gallery, keep it under observation without being seen. They were put in to protect us from theft."

So that was how he happened to see me.

"Was anyone in the office with you?"

"No. The clerks had left for the day."

"Did you see anyone in the foyer when you came out of that office?"

"No."

"How did you return to the room below?"

"By the lift." He pointed to the wall behind Martinique's desk.

"Then you saw Martinique alive at that time?" Duncan said eagerly.

"No. He was not at his desk. I left the memorandum for him. I had to wait for the lift. I went to the room below."

"What happened down there?"

"I looked about for Martinique. Miss Alvera came and said she was worried, that so many people had been storming in and out of the place. I told her that Martinique could take care of them and asked her where he was. She told me that he was in his office, that she thought . . ." He stopped.

"Just what did she think?" Duncan insisted.

"She said things seemed to be out of hand, Martinique was not himself, she was afraid he was ill."

"What did you do about that?"

"Nothing. It was none of my business. I told her he could take care of himself. I went about my work."

"And what did Miss Alvera do?"

"I suppose she came back here."

"What was the relationship between Martinique and Miss Alvera?"

I was glad he asked that question. It was something I wanted to know myself.

"Business."

"Was there any ill feeling between them today?"

"I wouldn't know."

His denial left considerable doubt in my mind.

"Miss Thomas has told me that a man made a scene this afternoon, that he was looking for his wife, that you came up here with him in the lift. Is that right?"

Enrico threw me a swift glance. "Yes, that is true."

"What happened to the man?"

"We sent him away."

"Did he see Martinique?"

"No. I convinced him that his wife was not here."

"Now what happened to the woman who claimed the gaming tables were crooked?" Duncan demanded.

"We sent her away."

"Who were those people?" Duncan asked.

Enrico gave him the names, which Crawford wrote on a slip of paper and handed to Duncan. "They were not here when it happened," Enrico said. "They had been gone for an hour or more."

"Since we do not know the exact time of Martinique's death, I don't believe we can dismiss those people," Duncan said pointedly.

"I saw Martinique alive after they had left."

"When?"

"On one of my trips up here."

"He must have been killed about the time you were up here," Duncan said slowly. "You saw Miss Thomas in the gallery: you saw Flannigan leave; you met Miss Alvera in the room downstairs. Where were the others? Did you see them at all, anywhere?"

Enrico had to think about that for a moment. "Miss Dodd had been here this afternoon. She was restless, angry at Martinique. She went up when I came down. . . . As a matter of fact it was she who was using the lift," he added.

"What about that lift?" Duncan demanded.

"It is an ordinary automatic elevator which can be entered from the hall in back of that wall, or from this room," he replied easily.

"What happened to Miss Dodd?" Duncan asked.

"I do not know. I was busy below. Miss Thomas came and asked to be shown the exit through the apartment building. Later Miss Dodd made the same request."

Duncan turned wide amused eyes on me. What did he know about that building? Was he trying to trap me?

"When was that?"

"Shortly after I had seen her in the gallery." Duncan grunted. "What about the others who are waiting outside?"

"It's so long ago," he said. "I remember seeing Miss Wayne, Mr. Bradley and Mrs. Wayne going up the stairs."

"Just when was that?"

"A few minutes before Miss Thomas came down and asked to leave by the side exit."

"Where do you suppose Martinique was when you were up there?" Duncan asked easily.

It was a trick question and I waited anxiously for Enrico's answer.

"I don't know. Perhaps Miss Alvera can tell you," he suggested.

"Call Miss Alvera," Duncan said.

"It's a fine puzzle," Tweed whispered. "Duncan suspects you."

"Don't talk to my witness," Duncan snapped.

CHAPTER EIGHT

ENRICO SETTLED into a chair somewhat removed from us and studied his hands which, at the moment, were folded in his lap. I was idly noticing that the dark suit was more becoming than the gray one he had worn in our encounter in the apartment building. As I was trying to determine whether he was a Spaniard or a Mexican, Miss Alvera came in. She walked up to Duncan and paused about three feet from him. Her eyes were hard and calculating as she waited. As far as she was concerned there was no one in the room but Duncan.

Miss Alvera stated that she was Martinique's secretary, that she had had a busy afternoon, that unusual things had happened, that people had been excited and angry.

"Be more specific," Duncan suggested.

She stated that Martinique came in immediately after lunch, in a blind fury. He had had some kind of an accident, there was a bruised spot on his chin. He told her to call Mrs. Wayne and have her come to the Gallery, which surprised her because he did not usually deal with mothers.

"What happened to make him so angry? Did he tell you?"

"No. He was too mad and determined. I heard him say, 'I'll show her she can't fly out here and interfere with my plans!'"

"Whom did he mean?"

"I think he referred to the old lady."

I had been expecting her to take a dig at me and it had come, sooner than I expected, and not too flatteringly. I listened as Duncan plied her with questions.

She said that Martinique had been surprised that I had arrived by plane, that in some way it seemed to interfere with his plans. I interrupted then and asked, "Are you sure he didn't mean Miss Dodd, or Miss French? They both arrived by plane with me."

"He expected Miss Dodd," Enrico replied quickly. "I went to the airport to meet her. We knew nothing about the arrival of Miss French."

"What about Miss Dodd?" Duncan asked.

They had no information to give him, nor did they seem to know anything about Alice French. They admitted that Alice had been a friend of Martinique's, that she had called on Martinique during the afternoon, that neither of them had seen her since.

Duncan's next statement surprised me. "Martinique reported a man as missing this afternoon, one Harold Dast. What do you know about him? How long has he been missing?"

Miss Alvera threw Enrico a quick questioning glance but he turned his head away. "I don't know about that," she finally said.

"Suppose you tell me what you know about Dast," Duncan suggested.

She shrugged, determined, I think, to throw the responsibility of that answer on Enrico's shoulders; she looked at him in such a way that he felt it necessary to speak.

"I can help you, Inspector," he said. "Dast was a young actor who curried favor with Martinique. He was here all the time. He was a friend of the French girl just mentioned; as a matter of fact, they lived together in one of the apartments next door." He looked at me and I fancied he spoke with some inner satisfaction. "Dast was here the other night with Mr. Bradley and Miss Wayne. I haven't seen him since."

That remark of his certainly threw Harold Dast right into our laps.

"This French girl, was she with the party?" Duncan asked.

"No. Just the three of them. They went to Dast's apartment."

I didn't like Enrico's implications. "How do you know?" I asked. "Did you see them enter the apartment?"

"No," Enrico replied smugly. "Dast asked to be let out through the apartment entrance. He said they were going up for a couple of drinks."

Duncan gave me a quick quizzical look, the corners of his eyes wrinkled. Instantly I was sorry I had stressed the point, had made any mention of the apartment. He was shrewd enough to know that I was interested. I didn't like it, didn't like it at all. The questions were taking a most unfortunate turn. The very thing I had lied to avoid would take place. The children were going to be involved.

"Have someone go to the apartment next door and locate a Miss French," Duncan instructed Chitter.

"She registered at the hotel this morning," I said without thinking.

"Check on the hotel," he said to Chitter.

An assistant came in with a memorandum which he handed to Duncan, who asked after reading it, "When did the Red Arrow messenger come with an envelope for Martinique?"

I think Miss Alvera was surprised by that question but it was only for a moment. "It was before the tragedy," she replied.

"What was in the envelope?" he asked.

"I do not know."

He seemed satisfied for the moment, for he went back to his original line before the digression. "You say Martinique was annoyed about Miss Thomas's arrival in Hollywood. Do you know that or was it just an impression?"

"Well, it was an impression but I knew."

"You are quite sure that his annoyance was not caused by the arrival of Miss Dodd or Miss French?" he insisted.

"He did not know about Miss French's arrival then. Later when I told him Miss French wanted to see him he said, 'What the devil is she doing in Hollywood?'"

"Then he was annoyed at her arrival?"

"I suppose so. Yes, I'd say it was a surprise."

"Tell me about this afternoon—say, an hour before the murder."

"Mrs. Wayne came and talked to Martinique. Mr. Bradley came asking for the old lady."

"You mean Miss Thomas?" Duncan asked. I was grateful to him for that. The Alvera person had had it in for me on sight; why, I did not know, but then I didn't care for her either.

"Yes."

"What happened to Mr. Bradley?"

"I do not know. He went downstairs."

"Who came after that?"

"Miss Wayne. She was very angry when she came out of Martinique's office. She and her mother had a long talk."

"But they did not leave?"

"No. I heard them say something about Miss Thomas. I had been trying to locate Miss Thomas. Also Mr. Flannigan. Then Miss Dodd came. Miss Dodd was with Martinique when Miss Thomas returned looking for Mr. Bradley."

"Go on."

"Miss Thomas went into his office."

"You said Miss Dodd was there too."

"She had gone in, yes."

"Did you go in at that time?"

"No."

"Did Miss Dodd come out?"

"I didn't see her."

"She went to the gambling rooms," I said. "Martinique told her to try her luck."

Duncan paid no attention to the side remarks. He listened, made mental notes as the stenographer's flying pencil raced across the pages taking it all down. "Go on, Miss Alvera. Tell us the rest of what happened."

"Just after Miss Thomas went in there Mr. Flannigan arrived. He left the door open behind him. I went to close the door . . ." Her hesitation was too calculated, too well timed to be as reluctant as she pretended.

"Go on," he urged.

"Mr. Flannigan and Miss Thomas were arguing with Martinique. Mr. Flannigan lost his temper, I thought he was going to strike him. He changed his mind and left the room."

"What did they quarrel about?"

"Miss Thomas.

Duncan flashed me a quick glance. His eyes seemed to say, Tut, tut, at your age! He made me feel like a young girl for a moment, there was subtle amused flattery in his glance.

"Did you hear much of the quarrel?"

"No. That was the end of it. Mr. Flannigan was ready to leave."

"What did Flannigan say or do as he left?"

"He said to Miss Thomas, 'You see how it is.'"

"How did Mr. Flannigan act?"

"Like a man who has been terribly beaten."

I will say this for the woman—her descriptions were graphic.

"Flannigan didn't threaten him?" Duncan asked.

"No. It was Miss Thomas who threatened him," she said devilishly as though she relished the statement.

"Tell me about that."

"Well, Martinique looked at her as Mr. Flannigan left and said, 'You see how it is. From now on you are in my hands.' Then she said, 'One of us will be dead first.'" She looked at Duncan, who was being a good audience. His eyes invited her to continue. Her voice took on a new tone as she went on: "She was furious, she came to the door, she pushed me out of the way, she stopped, and went back. I couldn't hear what she said because she leaned over the desk and slapped it with the top of her hand as she talked. She came away from him and at the door she said, 'Remember, in ten minutes, or take the consequences.'" She gave a very good imitation of me and my voice. She seemed to be boiling with anger only her boil was all bile.

"What did she mean about the ten minutes?" he asked.

"I don't know. She ran after Mr. Flannigan and talked to him for a few minutes. He came back and went into Martinique's office. I don't know what she said to Mr. Flannigan but he was a changed man. I was afraid. He brushed me out of the way."

"Then Mr. Flannigan was the last person to see Martinique alive. You told me it was Miss Thomas."

"I forgot," she said quickly.

"Testimony is important, Miss Alvera. You should be sure, and," he added, "you shouldn't forget."

"I was confused. All I could remember was her threats," she bit out.

"Did you hear anything while Mr. Flannigan was in there?"

"No."

"Did you listen?"

She looked up guiltily. "I tried. The door was shut and the room is soundproof."

"You know Martinique was alive when Flannigan went in?"

"Yes."

"You did not see him alive after that?"

"No."

"And as far as you know Flannigan was the last person to see him while he was alive?"

"Yes, but others must have been in the room."

"What others?"

"Miss Wayne and Mr. Bradley, and Miss Dodd."

"Did you see them go into the room?"

"No."

"Then how can you make such a statement?"

"Because I went downstairs looking for Enrico and I saw first Miss Dodd, then Miss Wayne and finally Mr. Bradley come out of the lift."

"Couldn't they have entered the lift from the hall?" I asked.

I was positive she was going to say, "No." Why she changed her mind I did not know but she finally said, "Yes, they could."

"Why did you want to find Enrico?" Duncan asked.

"I was worried."

"About what?"

"The succession of events. The angry people. The air seemed full of—well, danger!" she stated.

Either the woman had had an honest premonition of what was about to happen or she wanted to give that impression. I decided on the impression idea because I was biased against her from my first encounter. She was a hard woman and, I felt sure, a bad one.

"You have mentioned Mr. Flannigan, Miss Thomas, Miss Dodd, and Miss Wayne. Where was Mrs. Wayne during this time?"

"I do not know. She came into the foyer just after Mr. Flannigan went in for the second time. I told her she would have to wait. She was very angry at that."

"Just where was Miss Thomas at that time?"

"She stayed in the main gallery. She was there when I went for Enrico."

"How did you go downstairs?"

"By the lift from the hall," she answered.

"How long were you gone?" he asked.

"I don't know. Ten minutes at the most. Long enough for it to have happened." She actually glared at me as if she wanted to give the impression that I had killed him.

Duncan caught the implication. "Miss Thomas has an alibi for the time of the murder, I think," he added in a tone that I did not like.

I looked at Enrico. His face showed no expression whatever but his head did give a slight nod in agreement. He had given me an alibi of sorts for which I felt thankful.

Some one of us had killed Martinique in the few minutes that elapsed between Flannigan's re-entry into the room and my discovery of the body. I was trying to think of how it could have been done so quickly. According to the stories told by Enrico and Miss Alvera the equivalent of a parade had passed through the room. It seemed incredible that it could have happened without someone seeing the murderer or at least hearing the shot. Then I remembered that Miss Alvera had just stated that the room was soundproof. That would account for it.

"Tell me about finding the body," Duncan urged.

"Things had quieted down. Most of the people had left, the clerks had gone. I wanted to leave for the night. I tried to contact Martinique on the talk-a-phone. He did not answer. I tried to locate him in the rooms below. Enrico had not seen him. I became alarmed. I came in and found him sprawled out on the floor, a bullet through his heart."

She turned to look at me and ended, "That woman threatened his life."

"She's got the knife out for you," Tweed whispered.

"And so has he," I whispered back, for I realized that Duncan had an idea that I had lied to him about being in the room.

"Umm," Duncan mused. "He was dead, I think you said."

Her hard eyes snapped.

"I didn't say. I did not touch him. I was frightened. I called for help at once. I waited in the hall until Enrico came."

"You are sure that Martinique was alive when Flannigan went in the second time?" Duncan asked.

She hesitated.

"I think so, yes."

"When you went below, Mrs. Wayne was in the foyer and Miss Thomas was in the gallery, that right?"

"Yes."

"And you saw nothing more until later, after these people had all gone?"

"Yes."

"Now, Miss Alvera, Miss Thomas has stated that she did not enter the room again, that she merely peered through the open door, and since he was not at his desk she supposed he had left. She says she did not go in. Isn't it possible that Martinique was at the closet when she looked into the room? She would not have seen him if he were there, would she?"

"I saw her come out of this room, close the door, and move into the gallery to her friends. A few minutes later she came back and went downstairs. She must have . . ."

She stopped. I think she was going to accuse me openly and changed her mind.

I was accusing her in my mind. The story she told was logical enough but there was only her word for it. Before she went down she could have gone into the office via the lift, killed him and carried him to the closet. She was strong enough to have done that. With Martinique dead the rest of her story was simple enough. If she could make Duncan believe I had walked out of the room she would be safe and she knew it. Of course, I had walked out of the room, but how could she be so positive? Where was she? I had not seen her. She was not in the foyer. I decided she would need watching.

"How long were you alone after you discovered him?" he asked.

"It seemed like ages," she replied, giving the impression that the waiting had been a horrible experience.

"Did you kill him?" Duncan shot the question at her.

She recoiled as though stung. He had surprised her.

"No," she declared after a shocked moment. "Why should I kill him?"

"I can't answer that question," Duncan replied. "Of course, you must realize that you have no real alibi. You state that Martinique was alive when Flannigan went in there. From that time on your movements are unaccounted for . . ." She was about to protest but he silenced her. "I know you were downstairs, that you saw the other people, but you cannot prove that you didn't kill him after Miss Thomas and her party left."

Her hard eyes snapped fire. "I did not kill him. He was there on the floor, I told you." She lashed the words at him. "She could have killed him, she threatened him!" she cried, pointing her long fingers at me as her eyes snapped hatefully.

CHAPTER NINE

AS WE WAITED for Flannigan to come in, I wondered what new angle the case might take. Enrico had given me an alibi for part of the death time. Miss Alvera had practically destroyed that by declaring that I had left the room. Duncan's suggestion that Miss Alvera might have killed him after we left sounded all right but I knew that was not true. While Enrico had alibied me I could not do the same for him, nor any of the others, for that matter. Miss Alevera might have killed him after Flannigan left. That was a point I might make to Duncan later if the going became too difficult for us.

I regretted my unfortunate effort to shield the children. It would have been so much better if I had put myself on the side of the police from the very start. As always, hindsight is so much better than actual actions. I'd probably have difficulty now making Duncan believe me. I was contrary, however. I had made a mistake and instead of being intelligent about it and confessing at once I went on with the farce.

Flannigan gave me a well-here-we-are glance as he came in. His face was red, his manner nervous as he paused a few feet from the door and waited. It was like a parlor game we were playing. Each newcomer to the room wondered what had gone on, was decidedly uncomfortable under our glances.

After Flannigan had given his name and address he shifted his weight to his heels and seemed to be falling backward.

"You were the last person to see Martinique alive," Duncan said.

"That's my Irish luck," Flannigan replied, relieved, I think.

"It may not be such a piece of luck, since no one saw him after that. Can you prove he was alive when you left?"

"How could I prove that?" Flannigan demanded.

Duncan shrugged. "You might know of someone who saw him after you did. Do you?"

"I went back to my office. I didn't see anyone enter as I left."

"Did you kill Martinique?"

"No!" Flannigan bellowed the denial.

"You quarreled with him this afternoon," Duncan accused.

Flannigan threw me a hurt look but I think he caught my meaning as I glanced in Miss Alvera's direction. It was all very quick but not fast enough to escape Duncan's shrewd eyes.

"Don't try to get help from your friends. It makes for suspicion," Duncan warned.

"You know I had a row with him," Flannigan retorted.

"What about?"

"Miss Thomas's contract."

"Did you agree to give up that contract?"

"I did until I talked to Miss Thomas. Then I went back to tell him that I would not release her, that I would see him in hell first."

"So you sent him there, eh?" Duncan asked.

"I did not," Flannigan snapped back, "but that's likely where he is. He ought to be, at any rate."

"How did Martinique take your ultimatum?"

"He laughed at me at first. Then he said . . ." Flannigan paused.

"Go on," Duncan urged.

"Well, he said he'd forget everything for five thousand dollars. I turned him down. I was through with him."

"How long were you in here?"

"A few minutes, three or four, no longer."

"How did you leave this room?"

"By the regular door."

"Did you see Mrs. Wayne or Miss Alvera?"

"No. The only person I saw was Enrico. He was coming up, the stairs."

"But Miss Alvera has told us that she left Mrs. Wayne in the foyer waiting to see Martinique," Duncan said.

"I can't help that. I saw no one but Enrico on the stairs," Flannigan insisted.

"When you left Martinique had you every intention of keeping your resolve to defy him?"

"Yes."

"Then why did you call him on the telephone after you left? What did you intend to say to him?"

"Why—I—"

"You were worried, weren't you?"

"Yes."

"And did you intend to compromise?"

"No!" Flannigan looked at me as if he wanted me to believe him.

"And you maintain that he was alive when you left the room?"

"I do."

"I want you to answer this carefully," Duncan warned. "Was the door open or closed as you went out?"

Flannigan suspected a trap. He hesitated. I wanted to cry out, to urge him to tell the truth. I knew where Duncan was heading. He knew the knob of the door had been wiped clean of prints. Flannigan didn't know that. He must give the right answer, he must tell the truth.

"It was closed," he said after thinking about it. "Yes, I remember. I fumbled with the knob and he was still laughing at me. I yanked the door open and slammed it behind me."

Duncan glanced in my direction, a gleam of satisfaction in his eyes.

An officer came in and reported that they had been unable to locate Auriel Dodd. That was my moment but I let it pass. Things might have been different had I spoken then but I was so involved, so anxious to go on protecting the children that I was blinded, caught in the toils of my first lie and determined to carry on to the bitter end. How very near my end it came was due to my own sheer stupidity.

Duncan waved Flannigan toward a chair. Flannigan was relieved; he let an explosive sigh escape him as he sat down and ran a finger about the edge of his collar.

"Do any of you know anything about Miss Dodd and the time of the murder?" he demanded. No one answered.

"How about you, Miss Thomas? I believe you saw her in this room with Martinique."

I told him of our encounter, of Auriel's shocked surprise when she realized that Martinique had fooled her about the part, of her anger, and Martinique's suggestion that she go down to the gambling rooms until later.

"Did she go down?" he asked.

I shrugged at that.

"She came down—just when, I don't know," Enrico offered.

"What happened to her?" Duncan demanded.

Enrico thought for a moment. "She asked me about Dast, said she would like to see him. I told her that he lived next door but that I had not seen him for a day or so. She went into the apartment building."

"Did you see her again?" Duncan asked.

Enrico shook his head while I wondered why Harold Dast's apartment had been chosen for Auriel Dodd's rendezvous with the killer.

Duncan ordered the policeman to keep up the search for both Auriel Dodd and Alice French. After the man had gone he called Henrietta.

She made no effort to conceal her annoyance. While she gave her name and address I found myself wondering what had happened to Martinique just after Flannigan had left. I was inclined to believe Flannigan's story because he admitted leaving the room by the door into the hall. I felt confident in this day and age of motion pictures and mystery stories that Flannigan if guilty would have left no fingerprints as he quit the room. Just when had Martinique been killed and who had done it? Anyone might be guilty.

Henrietta waited. As she stood there, dignity personified, she made me think of one of Peter Arno's cartoons.

"Why did you come here today, Mrs. Wayne?" Duncan asked.

"Martinique sent for me."

"Why?"

"He wanted to marry my daughter. He demanded I give my consent," she answered, bristling with indignation at the very thought of it.

"You say he demanded."

"Yes, he did."

"And what did you say?"

"I told him I would have to think about it first, consult with my daughter."

"Were there to be penalities if you did not consent?" he asked.

Henrietta flushed. Her eyes were cold as she replied, "He threatened me."

"How?"

"He said he would ruin my daughter's picture career." She stated it rather convincingly I thought.

"Did he have proof that he would be able to do it?" Duncan demanded.

Henrietta's answer was quick enough but a shadow flickered across her eyes as they involuntarily went toward the desk. "He said he had proof."

"Did he show you the proof?"

"No." Henrietta's reply was stony.

"Had you reached a decision about the proposed marriage before you left this afternoon?" he asked.

"I had."

"Did you tell Martinique?"

"No. I didn't.

"Why not?"

"There was someone in his office when I had made my decision."

"Just what had you decided?"

"That I would not give my consent to such a marriage. I never wanted my daughter in pictures, anyhow," she said, with very anti-picture emphasis.

"You left Miss Thomas intending to talk to Martinique, did you not?"

"Yes, but the secretary person told me that Martinique was engaged."

"What did you do?"

"I waited a few minutes."

"Who was in the office with Martinique?"

"I've no idea."

"I thought you said you were waiting," he prompted.

"I didn't wait that long."

"Just where were you, Mrs. Wayne? Where did you go?"

Henrietta hesitated.

"Are you going to answer?" he demanded.

"If I must, yes. I went to the powder room."

I chuckled. She was so embarrassed I wanted to laugh.

It wasn't what Duncan had expected and left him rather flat for a moment, but not for long. "Did you see anyone during those few minutes?"

"No. Not until I saw my daughter and Mr. Bradley coming up the stairs and later met Miss Thomas in the gallery," she declared.

"Now, Mrs. Wayne. Did Miss Thomas come out of the room or was she at the door looking in?"

"I noticed her at the door," Henrietta stated without a quiver in her voice. Good old Henrietta, she didn't let me down!

"You left the gallery. Was Miss Thomas with you?"

"No. She said she'd meet us at the hotel."

He glanced at me before he said, "And you didn't see Martinique a second time?"

"No, my anger had cooled."

"So you were angry?"

"Of course I was angry. I was furious. I intended to tell him I would see my child dead rather than married to him." Her tone and glance were withering.

"Wouldn't it have been simpler if he died?" he suggested.

"It is more satisfactory this way," she admitted flatly.

"Was your anger at a fever pitch while you waited?"

"If you mean was I mad enough to kill him, yes. I might have done it the first time had we been left alone."

"Did you come equipped with a gun?"

"No, but I knew where there was one. I had seen a revolver in his desk," she stated boldly.

"Are you sure you didn't see him a second time?"

"Positive."

"There is an automatic lift opening into this room. Do you know where it is?"

"In the wall behind the desk," she replied honestly.

"Then you are familiar with its operation?"

"I'm intelligent enough to operate one, yes."

"Did you use the lift?"

"No. But I know where it is because when I was in here that man popped into the room and gave Martinique a memorandum." She pointed at Enrico.

"What did you do with the gun?" he asked.

"What gun?" she demanded.

"The one you took from Martinique's desk after you entered the room via the lift and killed him."

"Don't be ridiculous!" she snapped. "If I had killed him you don't suppose I'd be fool enough to tell you, do you?"

"No, I don't believe you would," he replied with a grin.

"Well then," she breathed. "Just because I was furious enough to kill him doesn't mean that I did. I don't know what I might have done if he had been alone when I went back," she ended.

CHAPTER TEN

HENRIETTA'S clear statement of her murderous intentions was a shock. I couldn't imagine why she made such a declaration, unless she was trying to shield someone else. Duncan would be more suspicious of Stella and Peter because of it. She should have realized that. Stella was called next.

Before her catechism began a man entered to say, "I have the proof of all the prints, Chief."

"That's fine, Martin, we've been waiting for you. Will you take the prints of these people while I go on with the questioning?" His glance swept over us. "You can refuse to be printed here. If you do, I'll have to take you to headquarters. It doesn't hurt, it's for your protection and until an arrest is made it is not a criminal record. If you are innocent, it can do you no harm."

After a speech like that there could be no doubt of our willingness to comply with his request. None of us wanted to seem more guilty than he had made us at the moment.

"There is no reason why any of us should object," I said. I crossed to the desk where Martin was unloading his equipment. He carried a little box from which he had taken his inking pad, his plate, a roller, and cards and, I noticed with appreciation, a bottle of cleaning fluid and some clean squares of cheesecloth.

"You're an old hand at it," Martin said as I went through the operations. I made no reply, for I wanted to hear Stella's answer to Duncan's first question, which was, "Miss Wayne, tell me why you came here this afternoon."

"I came looking for Mr. Bradley."

"And Mr. Bradley was looking for Miss Thomas. Was it a game you were playing?"

Stella smiled. "No. Mr. Bradley met Miss Thomas at the airport and took her to the hotel. I met them there. We were all tired and sleepy. I had gone into Miss Thomas's bedroom with her, leaving Mr. Bradley on the couch, nodding, barely able to keep his eyes open. We talked for a little while until I began to feel drowsy. The next thing I knew I woke up to find myself alone. I went out into the sitting-room to find it empty. Later I questioned the doorman, who told me that Miss Thomas had left by cab, that Mr. Bradley had followed her, so I came along."

"You saw Martinique when you arrived here?"

"Yes."

"Did you discuss your possible marriage with Martinique?"

"I wouldn't call it a discussion. I simply said no," she stated flatly.

"Why didn't you wait for Bradley and Miss Thomas at the hotel? What was the urgency, your haste, why did you follow them here?"

"I don't like being left behind."

"What did you think they were doing here?"

"I didn't know."

"Weren't you afraid that Mr. Bradley might do something desperate?" he demanded.

"No," she replied matter-of-factly.

"When were you in this room?"

"I don't know exactly."

"How did you leave it?"

"By the door."

"You are sure?"

"Yes."

That settled it. I knew then the point he was making but I could see no reason for his making it. "What did Miss Thomas say when she came out of the room just before you left?"

Stella didn't correct him. She accepted his statement as true that I had left the room. "'I'll meet you later,' or something like that," she answered.

"You left this room by the door, you said?"

"The first time I came in here, not the last time," she stated quickly.

"Oh. I didn't realize that you had been in here twice. Tell me about it."

"I wanted to find Mr. Bradley. I knew he was here somewhere because his car was parked outside. I came in here, but the room was empty. That time I went down in the lift over there."

"We are trying to establish the time of the crime." His tone was conversational. "In minutes, Miss Wayne, how long was it from the time you came through the room until you saw Miss Thomas come out of the room and you all started for home?"

"Ten perhaps, I don't know. While I was looking for Mr. Bradley, he appeared. We came back immediately after that."

"Call Mr. Bradley," Duncan ordered.

Stella crossed to the line in front of the desk to have her prints taken.

Peter's brow was troubled as he entered. He looked about, questions in his eyes. I tried to smile reassuringly.

"Now, Mr. Bradley, suppose we have your story," Duncan suggested.

"What do you want to know?" Peter asked. Duncan was interrupted by the arrival of a man with a report which he stopped to read.

When he looked up from the paper he said, "Tell me what you did this afternoon."

"I came down here looking for Miss Thomas," Peter replied.

"Did you find her?"

"Not at first. I saw Martinique, who told me that Miss Thomas had gone down to do some gambling."

"Did you go to the gambling rooms?" Duncan asked Peter.

"Yes. Miss Thomas was not there. Enrico told me that she had gone out through the other building. I followed but could not locate her."

"How did you return here?"

"Via the street. I walked around the block expecting to see Miss Thomas."

"And where exactly did you find her?"

"Out there in the main gallery waiting for the others."

"What others?"

"Mrs. Wayne and Miss Wayne."

"And where were they?"

"Miss Wayne was looking for me. I do not know what Mrs. Wayne was doing."

"You went into Martinique's office?"

"Yes."

"What was Martinique doing?"

"He wasn't there, no one was there. I thought they had gone below."

"When you entered the office did you close the door behind you?" Duncan asked.

"Yes, I think I did," Peter said after thinking about it carefully.

"How did you leave this room?"

"I went down by the lift."

"Then you are a familiar of the place?"

"No. I was never in this room before this afternoon."

"But you knew how to operate the lift?"

"Of course," Peter replied with a grin. "The only trick about this one is the spring in the paneling. I saw him operate it when I was here earlier this afternoon. It didn't seem to be a secret. Was it?" he asked.

"I don't know. There are other secrets here, more important ones. Tell me, why were you so anxious to find Miss Thomas?" Duncan demanded.

"Miss Thomas is new to Hollywood. I didn't want her involved with a man like Martinique," he replied promptly.

"Was there any reason why she should be?" Duncan asked pointedly.

"Martinique evidently thought so," Peter answered quickly. "She is to make a big salary out here that would make her attractive to a man like Martinique."

"And that was your only reason for trying to find her?"

"That was my reason," Peter repeated.

"Very altruistic of you, but not exactly complimentary to your fiancée," Duncan said sarcastically. "Did you care, weren't you angry, when you learned of the proposed marriage?"

"I didn't know about that until I came back and met Miss Thomas outside," he said honestly.

"Oh, I see," Duncan said. "You are sure you didn't see Martinique on your second trip?"

"Positive."

"When you met Miss Thomas in the foyer, where was she?"

"At the door of this room," Peter replied.

"Was she leaving the room or looking in?" he asked.

"Leaving," Peter answered.

Duncan smiled, quite satisfied with himself. "Another point I'd like you to clear up for me. Did you see Miss French?"

Peter was obviously surprised. "No. I didn't."

"Did you see Harold Dast?"

"No."

"Do you know why Harold Dast is missing?"

"No!" Peter almost shouted his denial.

I saw Henrietta squirm at the question, which worried me.

"When you were looking for Miss Thomas, did you go to Dast's apartment?"

Poor Peter! That question troubled him. I willed him
to deny any such visit but it was of no use. "I rang the
bell," he said.

"Why?"

"I just thought I'd see if he was in," Peter answered.

"Did you have an idea that Miss Thomas might be
there?"

"Why should she?" Peter demanded.

Duncan shrugged. "I wouldn't know. I was merely
asking."

"Miss Thomas had been gone from the gambling room
for a long time when I met her in the apartment
building," Enrico said to Duncan.

"How long?'

"I don't know, not in minutes. I let her out. Later I
went to my apartment. I was about to return here when
she slid down the stairs and bumped into me."

All eyes were turned in my direction. I caught Duncan
smiling. "Would you say it was five or ten minutes?" he
asked.

"I think it must have been more than that," he replied
after consideration. "Yes, it must have been more like
twenty minutes or a half-hour."

The fingerprints were all taken. Martin was collecting
the sheets and his equipment.

"Just where did you find Miss Thomas in the
apartment building?" Duncan asked Enrico.

"She slid down the stairs from the fourth floor. She
said she was trying to find the entrance to the gallery."

"Do you know the apartment building well?"

"I manage it," Enrico replied.

"He's putting the hooks into you," Tweed whispered.
"You'd better think fast."

"Then you know the location of Dast's apartment
there?"

"Yes."

"Was Miss Thomas near the apartment?"

"When we collided, yes. There had been some excitement in the building. I myself had heard a thud but I paid no attention to it. It might have been the rumbling of a truck. Some of the tenants from the floor below, however, thought it more serious. They were in the hall coming up. They insisted that I investigate. The door to the apartment was open."

"Oh, it was," Duncan said.

"Yes. I went in. The bed in the living-room had fallen out of the closet," Enrico explained.

"Did Miss Thomas go in with you?"

"No. She disappeared. I did not see her again until the officer brought her back," he stated.

The fingerprint expert had put away his equipment.

"I'm ready to check with you," he said. "We have the bullets too. How about the gun?"

"We haven't found that yet," Duncan said.

"Want me to frisk them?" Casey the policeman asked eagerly.

I was still being contrary. I should have signaled Duncan then and made a clean breast of it but I went on with my foolish idea of keeping him in the dark. I could have explained the bracelet quite easily but I was obsessed with the desire to shield the children and keep them, if I could, out of the scandal which was sure to follow the case. Casey's suggestion that we be searched startled me. Instead of being reasonable I tried to think of some way to get the bracelet out of my possession in the event of a search. It would mean more explanations.

"Not now. I'll keep you all here a little longer," he announced as he crossed the room. "Chitter, keep your eye on them. Come along, Casey."

He left us alone, which was a relief. The moment he had gone Enrico and Alvera began talking in Spanish. Before we could exchange any views or ideas, Chitter warned, "Hey, cut that out. If you want to talk, talk United States and give everybody a chance."

Tweed sitting beside me chuckled.

I was still worried about Casey's glib suggestion that we be frisked. I did not like the turn Duncan's questioning had taken. He was too interested in Harold Dast, that apartment and the French girl. I could not afford to have them find the bracelet on me until I knew more about Duncan and his plans.

Tweed squirmed in his seat. He was beginning to be bored. Tweed! They wouldn't search him. I would use the young man. He was quick, bright as the morning light, and probably quite unreliable, but I had no choice and I couldn't afford to be fussy at that time. I felt confident that he would do anything for a good story, even betray me.

I moved a little closer to Tweed. "I'm worried," I said in a low voice.

"Duncan is no fool. He's got an idea. The case is getting thick. You and your friends are on the spot."

"It's always darkest before the dawn," I replied. "Sometimes an ax has two edges."

He grinned. "Double talk, eh?" I nodded. "What do you want to tell me?"

"Nothing directly."

"I get you," he said softly because Chitter was watching us. "Want to play a game?" Tweed suggested brightly, and loud enough for all to hear.

"What game?" I asked.

"Bromides. You can pull 'em but I bet I know more than you do," he challenged. Then under his breath he said, "Maybe you can get your idea over."

"I've lived longer and heard more," I said, seizing upon the idea. It was the very thing. I knew the young man was bright. I could quite probably get my message across without Chitter suspecting us. It was worth trying.

"I'll bet you a fiver, that I can beat you at it."

"It's a bet," I agreed.

"A fool and his money are soon parted," he began, feeling a little proud of himself.

"That's because there's a sucker born every minute," I retorted promptly.

"You hit the bull's eye that time," he said with admiration.

"I've had a lot of practice."

"You need it. A liar should have a good memory," he said too pointedly, I thought.

"So you think there's more to this than meets the eye?" I questioned.

"I know it. I wasn't born yesterday. I always say you mustn't believe all you see and only half of what you hear. I'm one up on you now," he grinned. "No, that makes three."

"You're telling me. You ought to know that circumstances alter cases and much depends on where you sit. Some people are blind because they don't want to see." I grinned back at him. "That makes us even."

"You'd never give a hungry dog a bone, would you?" he asked.

"Perhaps Mother Hubbard's cupboard is bare," I suggested.

"What have you got up your sleeve?" he asked.

"It isn't in my sleeve, it's in my pocket," I whispered. "I want you to carry my burden for me. I've been casting straws to see how the wind blows."

He caught on at once. "It's an ill wind that blows nobody any good." His eyes actually danced. "Why don't you take a chance? An ounce of prevention is worth a pound of cure, you know."

"Well," I sighed, "beggers can't be choosers."

He waited a minute then said gleefully, "I'm two up on you; are you stumped?"

I giggled. He was so gay in that solemn group. Our senseless dialogue had been attracting too much attention.

"Cut out the double talk," Chitter said tersely. For an instant my heart stood still. Had that handsome hulk of rules and regulations seen through our game?

"I'll bet he'd be good at it," Tweed suggested.

"Cut it!" Chitter commanded.

"We're only playing a game," I said.

"It's a hell of a time to be playing games," Chitter grumbled.

"It's Bromides. Haven't you ever played?" Tweed asked.

"No!" Chitter said in disgust. "You make more noise than a barrel of monkeys. Pipe down!"

To his utter amazement we all laughed heartily—that is, all but Enrico and the Alvera woman. Even Henrietta smiled.

Tweed winked gaily at me. Chitter was angry, as people so often are when unconsciously they produce unexpected laughter in others.

"Break it up, you two," he ordered.

"But, Captain, we thought you were playing with us," I began.

"Me?"

"Yes. You see the idea is to think of all the trite and banal things that people say, such as old proverbs or time-worn expressions. You entered so into the spirit of the thing . . ."

"Well, I wasn't playing. Tell me what you mean," he insisted.

"It's like this: I say, I never let my right hand know what my left hand is doing." I had the bracelet in my hand and was withdrawing it from my pocket. As I spoke I nudged Tweed.

"Then I have to say one," Tweed chirped. "Let me see. I have it. A stitch in time saves nine."

"Then I say, Steve Brodie took a chance." Tweed had leaned closer but Chitter's eyes were on us.

"It don't make sense," Chitter said, "A lot of talk that means nothing." He relaxed, hitched up his trousers and brushed something from his sleeve.

I dropped the bracelet into Tweed's pocket and said, "Gold is where you find it."

Tweed caught that because he said, "There's a pot of gold at the end of the rainbow."

Chitter grunted in disgust.

"What's the dope? Can't you tell me more?" Tweed whispered.

My reply was a good poke with my elbow to silence him. Instead he said, "Ouch!"

"What's biting you now?" Chitter demanded.

"She poked me," Tweed replied truthfully like an aggrieved boy.

"Was he getting fresh, lady?" Chitter asked hopefully. "You can't give some guys any leeway."

"Oh no!" I said quickly. "I shifted and hit him with my arm. I guess my elbows are sharp."

"I'll say they are and that ain't all," Tweed replied.

"Discretion is the better part of valor," I returned. "We never know what is just around the corner."

"I know. Life is so strange. We two are like ships that pass in the night. When shall we two meet again?" he asked.

"Come up and see me sometime," I suggested.

"Then this is not the end?"

"No, the end is but the beginning," I replied. "And the first shall be last and the last shall be first."

"You win," I said. "I can't think of them as rapidly as you do." I dug into my pocket and brought out some bills. "Silence is golden," I said as I handed him five dollars.

"It cost you money," he remarked pertly, but I could tell by the glint in his eyes that he understood. I was greatly relieved.

It was then that I remembered that I was to get a call from Inspector Conklin from New York. Chitter was not at all sure that Duncan would agree to have the call transferred to me when it did come through. I explained to him quite carefully that the call would be put through to the hotel, that it could be transferred if the hotel knew of my whereabouts. At last he agreed to speak to Duncan.

It was arranged through the open door. Chitter came
back in and announced, "It will be all right, lady."

I would have been willing to place a bet on Duncan's
next move and yet when it did come I think I was as
much surprised as anyone. He came in looking quite like
the cat that had eaten all the goldfish. "I must ask you all
to wait outside," he announced.

CHAPTER ELEVEN

DUNCAN STUDIED me while the others were trooping out of the room. He sat on Martinique's desk with one leg swinging free. Finally he asked, "Were you ever arrested on a murder charge?"

I laughed. "No. I've always been on the other end."

"It's a good place to be. You're on the wrong end right now. It bothers me. I don't understand it or you."

"Things just look bad at the moment," I retorted.

"Let's take our hair down," he suggested. "Why did you come here this afternoon?"

"I was curious."

"About what?"

"Just curious. Like a cat."

"And you know what happened to the curious cat, don't you?" he asked.

"It was killed, wasn't it? You sound like Professor Quiz," I replied.

"You know things I should know, Miss Thomas. Things you ought to tell me. Will you?"

"I don't know you, Inspector, and although Inspector Conklin spoke very highly of you, still you are a policeman. If I knew a little more about you, if I knew what was in your mind, if I could be sure that you would not go off on the wrong tangent I might tell you my little secrets."

"Then you admit you have secrets?"

"No. You think I have. I admit nothing."

"Let's not hedge, Miss Thomas. This case is a mess. I'm not asking you for help—I'll get to the bottom of it eventually—but it takes time to discover the things that people could tell us if they only would." He paused for a moment. "I'm rather surprised at your attitude. You surely should know that the policeman of today is a reasonable human being. We don't try to make arrests just for the sake of making them. We don't want to waste our time on false clews. What we want to get in a case like this is the murderer."

"I know all that. You look for a motive first, then consider opportunity; when the two things fit you are inclined to think you have the right person."

"Not in this case," he said slowly. "I know that you lied to me about this room. You were in here. You knew that Martinique was dead. Why didn't a woman of your experience notify the police at once?"

"I thought that's what you were doing," I said. "You are a clever questioner, Duncan. I wondered what you would do when you satisfied yourself I had been in here."

"Then you do not deny it," he said.

"It would be useless. I stated that I looked into the room but did not see the body. You realized that I made a mistake right there. I could tell it from the quick shift of your eyes."

"Is my face as open as that?" he asked.

"I knew I shouldn't have said that the moment I had said it," I went on. "No one had ever mentioned the position of the body. My very statement told you that I knew the body was in a position so that it could not be seen from the door. That was a foolish mistake," I admitted.

"We all make mistakes." He grinned at me. "As a matter of fact, I didn't think of it from that angle until later."

"You mean after Flannigan admitted that he left via the foyer?" I asked.

"Yes. Of course, as you know there were no fingerprints on either of the door-knobs. If Flannigan was telling the truth he must have touched the knob. Who then had wiped the knob free from prints? Either you or the murderer. The murderer probably did not leave through that door, so you must have taken that precaution. You forgot something else. Your hand left a mark on the edge of the closet door. You wiped the handle but forgot the door edge. Why the precautions?"

"I didn't want to be connected with the case."

"And you were trying to protect your niece and Bradley. Do you think either of them killed him?" he asked.

"I am quite sure they did not. Nor Mrs. Wayne," I added.

"Then who did?"

"I don't know. On the face of it, it must be one of us and yet I know that we did not do it."

"What about Flannigan?"

"It's possible but doubtful," I said.

"What were your impressions of the man Enrico and Miss Alvera?" he asked.

"What would be their motive? I suppose either of them did have the opportunity," I conceded.

"You admit motives are important?"

"Of course. There haven't been many accidental murders," I replied.

"And I have a motive for the murder—this!" He reached back for a photograph and handed it to me.

It was the picture Martinique had taken that night in Harold's room. It was the evidence I had demanded Martinique return to me. I glanced at it. It was incriminating. There could be no doubt about the look of guilt on their faces as they looked down at the body at their feet.

"That," he said, "is the missing Harold Dast."

"And obviously a frame-up," I retorted.

"But doesn't it explain your connection with the case? Isn't that why they sent for you?"

"Yes."

"If it is a frame-up, why didn't they, or you, tell us about it at once?"

"You know the answer, Inspector. The average American fears the police, thinks of an officer as an ogre who will get him into all sorts of trouble. Imagine the terror of those children when Martinique told them that Harold Dast was dead."

"So that was his hold over them. Tell me about it."

I did. I told him the whole story just as Peter and Stella had given it to me. "You must realize how we felt. We would have called you eventually," I added.

"But you came here before calling us," he objected.

"What would you have thought of me if I had wandered into your office and told you such a story?"

"I'd have probably thought you were a very foolish old lady," he admitted.

"And you'd have been right too. I've told you what they told me. I believe it actually happened. You see how convincing Martinique must have been," I urged.

"They believed him."

"Remember they were under the influence of liquor, the thing had happened very suddenly, there was no time to investigate Dast's condition. Haven't you ever felt guilty yourself?" I asked.

He smiled slowly. "Often."

"Then you must know how they felt. The next day they were terrified when Martinique told them he had disposed of the body."

"But you didn't think he did?" he asked.

"No. The story smelled to high heaven, as you must admit. That's why I went to the Dast apartment, where I found this." . . . I dug into my pocket and produced what I had found near the couch, the wadding from the shell of the blank cartridge which was fired in that ugly frame-up.

"What made you look for that?" he asked.

I told him about the wilted cactus and the gin-soaked earth in the flower-pot.

"Nice work, Miss Thomas," he commended. "Very nice work!"

I went on then and told him about Alice French and Auriel Dodd's unexpected death.

At first he was furiously, explosively, angry and he let me know it. As he talked he became more reasonable and finally said, "That was a horrible experience. You must have nerves of iron to have stood it all."

"I have no nerves—much," I added. "I was worried about Stella and Peter."

"Then you were afraid of what they might do?"

"Of course I was afraid," I admitted. "The boy is very much in love."

"And when he learned that Martinique wanted to marry Miss Wayne he killed him," he said. "Is that what you thought?"

"Now you're talking like a dime novel detective," I challenged.

"It sounds like a dime novel," he reminded me.

"Except for the fact that Bradley did not know about the proposed marriage until I told him a few minutes before I found the body."

"But you don't know who killed him."

"No," I had to admit.

"If Bradley killed him, then Miss Wayne would lie to save him."

"Naturally," I agreed.

"Or if she had killed him, he would lie for her."

"Certainly. But where did either of them get the gun?" I demanded.

"That brings us to a point of believing your story," he said slowly. "I think you would lie to save both of them."

"Of course I would," I snapped, "under such circumstances. So would you if the situation were reversed."

"I'm beginning to have a change of opinion," he said, "but before we leave our little group I want to ask you something. You heard the questioning this afternoon. You believe your friends were telling the truth. Have you any idea when the murder was committed?"

"It's purely a guess on my part but I felt it at the time. It was an impression, a hunch if you will. I believe Auriel Dodd was close to the murderer."

"Then you believe she was killed because she knew too much?"

"What other explanation can there be."

"Which ought to put the murder in Flannigan's lap," he mused.

"Not necessarily. Flannigan's story rings true. Remember he admitted leaving by the door."

"Yes, that's right. If he had left the body in the closet, he would have been less direct in his testimony," he conceded.

"What about Harold Dast?" I insisted. "I don't believe the man is dead. It seems to me that he is the only person who has a motive for both crimes, unless . . ."

"Unless what?"

"Doesn't it seem strange to you that Miss Alvera waited so long before she found the body? If she was as upset by the afternoon's proceedings as she says she was, why didn't she try to contact Martinique sooner?"

"That's a point," he agreed.

"And Enrico," I went on. "He knows so much and so little. He was able to tell you about our movements. He is the only person who knew where Auriel Dodd went. Why did he go back to the apartment? Why did he change his clothes?"

"Perhaps that's why he went back there," he suggested.

"He did his best to point suspicion toward me. I don't trust the man, I don't know why. He met Auriel Dodd at the airport. He was annoyed with Martinique because of my entry into the affairs. Martinique reprimanded him severely. Mrs. Wayne has told us that Enrico popped into the office with a memorandum. If any one person in this place knew everything that was going on, Enrico is the man. He was up here. Isn't it strange that he should have seen so much and yet no one saw him?"

"Have you changed your mind about Harold Dast? Are you suspecting Enrico or Miss Alvera instead?" he asked.

"No. Dast is definitely involved."

"But if Dast killed her he wouldn't report himself missing, would he?" he demanded.

"No."

"Then the man who killed Martinique also killed Auriel Dodd. He reported Dast missing to throw suspicion on him. It's part of the plan," he argued.

"Just the same, I'd like to find Harold Dast," I insisted. "Also Alice French."

"The report says that Dast disappeared with funds belonging to Martinique," he explained. "Perhaps Miss French knows about that."

"And I still think you ought to find Dast."

"Doesn't your experience tell you that he is too obviously a wrong scent, a red herring?" he demanded.

"Fish or no fish," I snapped, "Dast must have been familiar with Martinique's plans."

"What plans?"

"I don't know. Dast and the French girl had been used by him. It is my belief that he intended to get rid of them and use Stella and Peter."

"Would he suggest marriage to Miss Wayne if that were the case?"

"That has puzzled me. I can't understand it. I have a feeling that getting married was a new development."

"Do you really believe Bradley and Miss Wayne are innocent?"

"I know they are."

He smiled at my sureness. "I've been wrong before."

"They are innocent, Inspector," I insisted.

"Did you know that Bradley tried to contact Miss French this afternoon at the hotel, that he asked the doorman about her and when he learned that she had come here, he followed her?"

That was a blow. Why, oh why, didn't they remain sleeping peacefully.

"I thought he followed me. If he was interested in her it was because he hoped to learn something about Dast," I assured him. "These two murders are connected in some way, Inspector, but not through Peter Bradley. There is a deeper motive underlying this case than we see on the surface. You'll have to dig into Martinique's business, you'll have to learn what he did."

"I think he was burning his bridges behind him, planning an escape," he said.

"Escape!" I was thoroughly surprised.

"Yes. Martinique was going away tonight—by plane."

"Where?"

"New York, first, after that, destination unknown."

"But . . . Why, that changes everything!" I cried.

"Does it?"

"Doesn't it?" I demanded. "Were there two plane tickets?"

"No. Just one."

"Then he had no intention of marrying Stella! All this was a smoke-screen behind which he had hoped to hide."

"What his reason may have been we cannot know."

"You still want to pin the murder on them, don't you?" I accused.

"Not necessarily. I believe that where there is smoke there must be some fire. I don't want to arrest an innocent person. At the same time I cannot ignore the weight of circumstantial evidence which has piled up against them. Fear like theirs is an understandable motive for murder. They were cornered and were looking for a way out."

"Auriel Dodd was cornered. Dast is cornered now," I said.

"And your friend Flannigan?" he suggested.

"Had reached a point where he was going to stand on his own."

"All very interesting but it does not help your friends very much. I won't arrest them yet but I am going to hold them a little longer while I look into the killing of Auriel Dodd."

"By all means," I agreed.

"I've discovered something that will interest you. Alice French was called back to Hollywood by a telegram signed by Dast, but it was sent from here," he explained.

"And Miss Alvera says Martinique was surprised to learn of her arrival," I reminded him.

"Right," he admitted.

"And that ticket for the plane. Are you sure it was for Martinique?"

"The company says so. He ordered it this afternoon."

"But, Inspector! Suppose someone, Dast, for example, had planned Martinique's death. Was there anything to prevent him from ordering the ticket in Martinique's name?" I asked.

"No, but your line of thought starts a whole new chain of 'ifs and ands,' ramifications I don't believe we need. It would have been too risky a thing for Dast to have done."

I didn't believe him but I didn't argue.

"I've got to see how the French girl hooks into all this," he said.

"What will you do first?" I asked.

"Hunt for Auriel Dodd's body," he said grimly.

"How about Martinique's affairs, what are you going to do about them? Surely Enrico or the Alvera woman must know about his plans. They know more than they are telling. He couldn't have operated without one or both being pretty familiar with what he was doing. That photograph is not the only one of its kind, Inspector. Why should a man like Martinique hold this town in the palm of his hand? Why was Flannigan afraid of him? There must be a hiding-place somewhere in this building that will answer all the questions."

"We will find it," he promised.

There was a tap on the door. Casey stuck his head in to say that my New York call was coming through.

"She can take it in here," Duncan said. "Have it put through." As he walked to the door he said, "It isn't that I don't trust you, Miss Thomas; it's just that I don't believe in taking any chances. I'll send Chitter in to keep you company. I'm going to hold your friends a little longer."

I lifted the receiver and waited. Before the connection was completed Chitter came in.

"Are you ready, Ethel?" Conklin asked with that warm Irish chuckle in his voice.

"Yes," I replied.

"Your friend Dast has no police record. Disappointed?"

"No. Didn't you get anything at all?"

"Now take it easy," he laughed. "I've been through the newspaper morgue. There are a few bits."

"Then get on with it. This is an expensive conversation," I reminded him.

"The Dast family is socially prominent, or was."

"I never heard of them," I said.

"They may not be in the Blue Book but they got in the papers, pictures of Harold with debs, Harold at Southampton and Newport, Harold at Yale, Harold taking the feminine lead in a Yale show. He went there to take the dramatic course.

"What else?"

"Notices of Harold in Broadway plays. Harold was married to a show girl but his mother had it annulled."

"Who was the girl?"

"Auriel Dodd—that mean anything?"

"A great deal. Thanks! Go on."

"There's another bit. The Dasts were robbed about a year ago. Some fine old family jewelry was taken. The jewelry was never recovered."

"Go on," I urged as he paused.

"That's all there is. Does it help?" he asked hopefully.

"No. Not at the moment. How about this Dodd girl? Did you think to check on her?"

"I did. Just an actress. Doing well too."

"Nothing else?" I asked disappointed.

"What's it all about?" he asked eagerly.

"I can't tell you over the telephone." Then I had an idea. "Any chance of your coming out here, all expenses paid?" I asked.

"Can't be done, sorry. Is it murder?"

"I can't tell you anything yet and remember you have never heard about this lad or my connection with him."

"Mum's the word. Remember, if you need help, get in touch with Duncan of the Los Angeles force. He's a good man, just tell him you're a friend of mine."

"I did that very thing. I've just been talking to him."

"Then you don't need me. Give him my regards."

"I will. Goodbye."

As I started to replace the receiver I heard him saying, "Since this is not official business I'm reversing the charges. Don't let it keep you awake."

The line went dead.

So Auriel Dodd had been married to Harold Dast! What a spider Martinique had been, spinning webs into which he caught people who were closely connected. Did he want Dast out of his picture because Auriel Dodd was entering it? What did Auriel know about Dast at this time? Was Martinique really planning to leave Hollywood for good as Duncan seemed to think? Could it be possible he had planned to leave all that he had built? It did not seem credible. What had Auriel Dodd known about the killer? Would Dast know the same thing? If he did, wouldn't he come forward and tell the police, ask for their protection?

Who was the woman who had threatened my life in this very room? Why did she want the bracelet? I realized then that I had failed to mention the bracelet or the woman to Duncan in our talk. I had not intended to keep the facts from him. The progress of our talk from question to answer, his clever seeing through my attempt to conceal the fact that I had been in there with the body, had thrown that out of my mind.

I crossed to the wall in which the lift was so cleverly concealed by the panels. I was firmly convinced that the secret to the murder lay hidden there somehow.

I felt the molding. If that wood could only talk! Chitter was watching me. "Why don't you smoke or do something," I said.

"Don't be jittery, lady. He ain't locking up your friends yet." He produced a crushed packet of cigarettes and offered me one.

"So he told me," I replied. "He's a smart man."

"He sure is." Chitter breathed admiration with his smoke.

I felt an urge to do a little investigating on my own. Chitter, however, was a handicap unless I could use him. He was so conventional about his rules and regulations that I doubted my ability to win him over to any scheme of mine. There was one thing I wanted to know. How did Martinique get into the Dast apartment that night? How had Miss French arrived so silently, and the person who had killed Auriel? How had he entered?

"I suppose you'd like to be an inspector," I suggested to Chitter.

"I would. It's a swell job."

"I suppose Inspector Duncan is above reproach?" I asked.

"What do you mean, lady?"

"I understand this town has its share of rotten politics. A place like this must have had police protection," I stated.

"I don't know nothing about that," he said quickly.

"Is open gambling legal in the city?"

"No, ma'am, it isn't."

"But this was a gambling house."

"I don't know nothing about it," he denied.

"Are you an honest man?" I asked bluntly.

"Sure I am."

"Would you like to move up, get a better job?"

"Sure. I'm studying all the time."

"This case will be sensational. The man who solves it is going to be a big man in police circles. When things start to come out there will be a lot of wires pulled, some men broken, some jobs lost and advancement for the men who were honest and had the courage to see the thing through."

"What are you getting at?"

"I want to do a little investigating on my own. Will you work with me or must we sit here and waste time?"

"I had orders to keep my eye on you," he said.

"Then we could look around, as long as we were together," I suggested.

"I suppose so. Where do you want to look?"

I tapped on the wall behind Martinique's desk. "This lift interests me." He came and stood at my elbow until I located the piece of molding which worked the door. The panel slid open, I stepped inside, he followed.

"Where are we going?" he asked.

"Down to the gambling room."

The lift was a simple box done in some soft blond wood. The operating panel was on the rear wall as we stepped in. I pressed the button and down we went.

I was utterly amazed at the sight which met my eyes. The room I had seen before had completely vanished. There was not a gaming table in sight. Instead the room was furnished with heavy pieces of furniture and looked like a supplement of the show room upstairs. I had heard of such transformations but had never expected to see one.

"This is where they were gambling," I said as I looked about the room.

"Here?" he queried.

"Yes, right here. I'd like to know how they make the change."

"It looks kosher," he said.

"The walls are probably hollow," I said. I turned back to the lift.

"Funny, that room, ain't it?" he said as we started up again.

"Very," I replied, disappointed because of my little foray.

"What?" he fairly shouted. I don't know what would have happened if he had whispered as I had done. It may not have made any difference; I don't know. The car stopped but the door did not open in front of me as I had expected. That was what it should have done. I heard something slide behind me and the next moment there was a sickening thud and a grunt of surprise from Chitter. I felt that tower of strength crumpling behind me.

"Keep still," the voice belonging to the arm with the bracelet warned, "unless you want the same dose. Don't turn around, just reach into your pocket and toss the bracelet back to me."

I was both shocked and startled. Where had that person been all the time?

I hesitated. At my back was probably the solution to the mystery, at my feet was a man struck down, perhaps killed. Upstairs somewhere, Stella and Peter sat with a murder charge dangling over their heads. I banged on the wall of the car in front of me hoping that Duncan or someone would hear the noise. "Help! Help! He! . . ." I heard my third call die as I sank into oblivion.

CHAPTER TWELVE

I HAD BEEN KNOCKED senseless once before but it was nothing like this experience. As I began to regain consciousness my head felt like a giant ball attached to my body. Every inch of its increased size ached and throbbed. I tried to sink back into forgetfulness but the pain kept me awake. I remembered nothing, was aware of nothing but pain for the first few minutes. I seemed suspended in space, floating with my aching head. Then there was an upheaval beneath me and for a moment I seemed to be tossing on a heavy sea. My head ached unbearably. Could it be that I was in a boat and about to be seasick!

From somewhere far off there came the sound of tortured moaning. I listened. Was it I? Was I an astral body consigned to space? The moaning grew louder. I fingered my lips. They were still but the sound increased. My hand went up over the vastness of my skull and encountered a great lump. The heaving became turbulent, a great surge tossed me to one side and my poor aching head banged into something hard and unresisting. Stars scattered before my eyes. The new, sharp, sudden pain jerked me to my senses so that I realized what was going on. The heaving had been Chitter, on whom I had fallen. He was coming to from the blow he had received.

His arms thrashed out. I slid back out of their way and spoke to him. He managed a sitting posture and asked dazedly, "Was it an earthquake?"

"Yes, a female one," I replied as I gently rubbed the egg-shaped decoration on my head.

"Huh?"

"Never mind. Are you all right?"

"I guess so." Chitter was a little slow on the uptake. He looked at me in bewilderment for a moment. "I got you," he said finally. "You think it was a dame. No dame could pack a wallop like that."

"There are dames and dames," I replied. "Are we going to sit here all night?"

"Did you get hit?" he asked without moving.

"Look!" I bent forward to show my decoration.

"That's a honey," he said admiringly. "Does it hurt much?"

"It doesn't feel good," I snapped. "Come on, can you get up?"

We were a sorry pair when we struggled to our feet. We were both dizzy and clutched at the walls for support. We were at the mouth of a long narrow corridor. The thin light from the lift shone down upon us while we were on the floor. Chitter's great, leather-incased leg had held the lift door open. When he stood up the panel slid shut leaving us in total darkness.

"It's dark, ain't it?" he said.

"Very. Do you have a flashlight?"

"Yes, ma'am."

"Then let's get going. We ought to find something interesting."

"We'd ought to go back and tell Duncan," he said.

"Go back where?" I demanded.

"In the elevator we just left. This may be important," he suggested.

"And so is this corridor. What could we tell Duncan now except our troubles? Let's get something to talk about! Come on." I swayed against him.

"How about that noggin on your head?" he asked solicitously, and flashed his light over my face.

"It can wait."

"How are we going to get out of here?"

"Let's not worry about that, let's see what we can find. This third entrance to the lift is an important discovery."

"You certainly are game, lady. I got to hand it to you."

It was an honest compliment. I liked him for it. "Lead on, Macduff," I said.

"What?"

"Never mind. It's all right. Go ahead, and remember, I've just been hit on the head."

"Yes, ma'am. I knew a guy that got a blow like that and he's been kind of cracked ever since. You ought to be careful," he advised.

His soberness made me laugh. It did us both good, that bit of a laugh.

We started down the corridor. I've no idea how long it was but it seemed endless. There's no use pretending, I was afraid yet thrilled at the same time, wondering what we would find. I thought secret passages went out with modern building methods.

Chitter paused and turned the flash back on me. "Can you stretch your arms out and feel the walls?" he asked.

I found that I could.

"Good," he said. "I'll walk ahead. If you feel any irregularity let me know and we'll stop to investigate."

Bless the man! That was something that had not occurred to me. Except for his forethought we might have gone blindly on to the end of the passage. We had walked about half the distance when my fingers located a break in the wall. We halted before a door flush with the surface. Chitter handed the flash to me and took his gun. He kicked the door open and stepped back. From the edge of the door I played the flash into the room. I was careful, expecting the thing to be shot from my hand, but it was not. The room was dark and quiet.

"Come out!" Chitter ordered.

We waited but there was no sound within the room. "The bird has flown," I said.

"Is that one of them bromides you and Tweed was talking about?" he asked unexpectedly.

"It is," I replied.

"I thought so. Play the flash inside till I take a look."

As I flashed the light in and across the room he whistled. The next moment he had found the light switch. "Strike me down!" he exclaimed.

His bulk prevented my seeing what it was that had caused his whistle and exclamation. I peered around his elbow. No wonder he had been so excited. Auriel Dodd's body lay on a wooden counter in front of some cupboard doors.

Chitter moved forward. "She's been shot," he said. "Looks like it went right through her heart too."

I made no comment. Poor child, I knew all about her death.

"Come on! We got to get out of here! We got to tell Duncan about this!" he said, excited.

"Wait. How did she get here?" I asked.

"Someone brung her," he stated.

"Yes. But how? Let's have a complete story before we go back to Duncan. There's no point going off half-cocked, is there?"

"I don't get you," he replied, puzzled.

"She wasn't brought here through the gambling room or Martinique's office," I said. "Let's finish with this passage and learn where it leads us."

"Well, all right," he agreed reluctantly, but he did not move. He looked from her body to me and demanded, "How do you know how she got here?"

That was a good question and one which started me thinking but like so much hasty thought it started me on the wrong tack. That was because I had begun to form a theory which seemed the logical answer to the whole problem. That arm that had wanted the bracelet, this latest attempt to get it, both points seemed to coincide with the conclusions I had already made.

"Come along," I urged.

"I hate to leave her like that," he said, with an awed reverence for the dead, as he went into the passage ahead of me. We moved on as before, Chitter leading the way with a flash. In a few minutes we came to a dead end. "It's as far as it goes," he said.

"There have been no breaks in the wall since that room," I stated. "There must be an exit somewhere."

I crowded in beside him and together we manipulated the wall in front of us until we found a spring which released a catch. The wall slid to one side. We found ourselves facing a line of clothing hung on a bar. We were entering the back of a closet filled with men's suits and women's dresses. "Careful," he warned as he bent down to get under the clothes.

We went through the closet and found ourselves in an unoccupied bedroom. I looked at Chitter and laughed. In his passage through the closet he had become entangled in a thin, flimsy dress which was draped rakishly over one shoulder, and clung as he tried, to disentangle himself.

"What's so funny?" he demanded as he continued to struggle to free himself from the clinging material.

"You."

I know that men dislike being laughed at, but I could not help it. He was so funny.

"You look as if you came out of a ragbag yourself," he grumbled.

I took one look in a long mirror. How right Chitter was! My clothes were pretty much torn off me. My bodice was ripped and the pocket of my skirt was inside out. That was the first time I had thought about the money. Of course, it was gone. Our assailant had taken it when she looked for the bracelet. Well, the bracelet was safe for the time being, thanks to Tweed. How desperate the woman must have been to risk police capture to get at that bracelet! I dismissed the money as I looked again in the mirror. The lump on my head stuck out rakishly. There was a scratch on my neck that had bled a little. I had been turned inside out. She had known where to look and had wasted no time, just ripped away at every likely hiding-place. She had made a good haul. Four thousand dollars is a lot of money.

I shrugged and quoted to my reflection, "Who steals my purse steals trash—"

Chitter looked at me with disgust and said, "You know, sometimes I think you're real smart and the next minute I'm wondering if you ain't a nut."

"A little of both, well seasoned," I replied. "Let's go on. There's nothing here."

I fixed my clothing as best I could, tried to rub away the stain that had been there all afternoon.

"Looks like blood," Chitter said.

"Nonsense," I retorted and swung about.

As we went into the little hall I knew at once where we were. We were in Dast's apartment and one of the things I had wondered about was explained. I knew how Martinique, Alice French and the man who had killed Auriel Dodd had gained such easy access to the apartment. "Just a minute," I said and went back to that clothes closet.

A number of things began to take shape in my mind. Chitter had said that no woman could pack the wallop which had knocked him out. Was he right? Inspector Conklin had said that Dast had played leading feminine roles in college plays. Could it be?

Chitter stood in the door and watched me as I took several dresses from the bar and held them up against me and then compared them for sizes.

"Listen, lady, this is no time to try on dresses," he complained with uncontrolled disgust.

"Keep quiet," I snapped.

There were definitely two sizes of dresses in that outfit and the larger sizes were on the same end of the bar with the man's clothes.

I grew elated. I had to be right. Suddenly the whole truth unfolded itself. It was theory but there was no other explanation. I had been troubled up to that moment by the disappearance of Harold Dast. Where had he gone?

Where had he been hiding for two days? In a sense he had not been hiding. He had simply changed his clothes for one of the gowns hanging on the rack. For two days he had been masquerading somewhere as a woman, quite probably in that very apartment. No. That couldn't be right. He had been somewhere else. Alice French had not known where he was. She had been worried about him. She had half believed my story about the jewelry. In desperation, after waiting for him, she had come to the apartment. Had he double-crossed her after all? What was the pressing need which had brought him first to the apartment and later to Martinique's office for the bracelet?

By then there was no doubt in my mind that the arm that had tried to get the bracelet from me had belonged to Dast. But why had he risked so much? Why had he wanted the bracelet so badly? He knew Martinique was dead. He saw the body tumble from the closet. He must have known about Auriel Dodd. Did he know who had killed her? Had he killed them both? I was glad then that I had not mentioned the bracelet to Duncan. He was so full of doubt about the children, was so determined to believe them guilty. Now I held an ace in the hole, the bracelet. Why was it so important to Dast?

"Well?" Chitter demanded as I dropped the dresses on the bed.

"Let's go," I suggested, evading an answer. I went into the little hall and opened the door to the main corridor.

"We'd better look at the other rooms as long as we are here," he said.

"Go ahead, if you like. I'm going out."

"Then I'm going with you. I was told to keep my eye on you," he said, doggedly determined to stick to his orders.

"And a good job you've been doing," I approved.

"Don't be sarcastic," he said. "I wouldn't of let you get hurt if I hadn't been surprised."

"I'm not being sarcastic, Chitter. Heaven forbid! Our little accident was unavoidable." I patted his arm. I had grown fond of that great, not too bright, hulk of a man. He was gentle and kind as big people so often are. He clumped beside me as we went down the steps to the second floor.

We were faced by a group of police coming up. "If they ask you any questions, tell them you are taking me for a walk, Duncan's orders," I whispered.

"We hadn't ought to be going for a walk," he objected.

"We are not going for a walk," I snapped, annoyed by his literal interpretation of all remarks. "We are going back to Martinique's and we might as well go this way."

"Hello, Chitter," one of the approaching men called. "What are you doing?"

"Keeping my eye on this lady for Duncan," he replied.

As soon as the men had gone on up I opened the door leading to the erstwhile gambling room. "Another one of them secret passages?" he asked dubiously.

"Yes," I agreed. "Used in case of a raid. They do have raids out here, don't they?"

"Yes, ma'am. Every once in a while there's a raid."

"And I suppose the gamblers are warned," I suggested.

"I wouldn't know about that."

"No, I don't suppose you would," I agreed.

We reached the salon. "Looks innocent enough from down here, don't it?" he asked.

I nodded agreement.

"You'd have made a swell detective, Miss Thomas, but I guess you've been pretty good at whatever you've been doing," he said.

We crossed again to the wall which concealed the lift. I pressed a button and the whirring of the motor sounded.

"You ain't gonna take another chance in that, are you?" he asked.

"Lightning never strikes twice in the same place," I reminded him.

"But it does," he replied seriously. "Churches get hit over and over."

"And this is a long way from being a church," I retorted as we stepped into the car and the panel glided into place.

A moment later we were in the upper hall. We found Duncan snapping orders.

"Find them!" he was saying. "I tell you I left them in that room!"

"Do you mean us, Inspector?" Chitter asked with irritating brightness.

"Yes, my beamish boy," Duncan growled. "Where have you been?" Then he had a good look at us and his eyes twinkled at sight of my bedraggled condition.

"We've been making discoveries," Chitter replied proudly.

"What?" Duncan made no effort to conceal his contempt.

Chitter was agog to tell the story and I was too full of my ideas to have sense enough to curb him. I was rather proud of myself and wanted to bask a little in the light of accomplishment. I should have stopped Chitter but foolishly I didn't. He told the full story of our adventure as the entire group of suspects listened attentively. They were all there except Barnaby Tweed.

"Who attacked you?" Duncan asked when Chitter had finished.

"It had to be Harold Dast," I replied. "He was married to Auriel Dodd at one time. He must be the person who killed Auriel Dodd after he had killed Martinique."

"Did you hear him speak?" Duncan asked quickly.

"No."

"And you didn't see him?"

"No. How could I, hidden as I was behind that closet door?" I demanded.

"There may be something in your idea," he agreed.

"Of course there is. It has to be," I insisted, and added, "Surely you are not going to hold us now?"

"Why not? Do you think the finding of the body and the attack on you is any excuse to let you go?"

"Of course it is. These people were with you, weren't they? None of them could have rapped us over the head, you know."

The man hesitated. I knew later that he had had the right idea but I was so full of my own theory, my story was so logical, things had happened so fast that I completely forgot about the bracelet.

Had I told him about it then, the story would have been different. In my mind Dast loomed so logically as the killer because of the fraud in his apartment connected with Peter and Stella, the attack on us, his method of remaining in hiding, the fact that he had been married to Auriel—all that loomed so importantly that the bracelet was a minor incident which I glossed over, not purposely. Had Tweed been in the room I might have thought about it, but I didn't.

"I'll let you go," Duncan finally said, "but don't any of you try to leave town, remember that. I'll probably want you all again."

There were sighs of relief as the suspects moved away.

Peter stood beside me.

"You pulled us out of a tough hole," he said, relief in his voice. "The Inspector learned about the row at the hotel and thought that was important enough to hold me."

"I'll remember it," Duncan warned.

"Come along," I said.

As we walked out of the hall toward the gallery Duncan called after us and I know he meant me, "Don't pull any fast ones just because I'm letting you go."

CHAPTER THIRTEEN

HENRIETTA WAS scandalized by my appearance. When I insisted that it would do until I reached the hotel she put her foot down. "You are not going back to the hotel looking like that, you are not going back to the hotel at all," she added. "Peter can go get your things while I take you home with us. Now fix yourself so that you will be halfway presentable—after all, one must consider the servants."

I was perfectly willing to allow myself to be browbeaten. I had been through more than enough for one day. I was tired and I was hungry. I thought wistfully of a warm bath, a tray in bed with a lamb chop, a fluffy baked potato, a green salad with roquefort dressing, hot coffee and then, sleep. Since the children were not under arrest the question of who killed Auriel Dodd and Martinique was purely academic. I did not care as I tried with the aid of a few safety-pins to make myself presentable enough to satisfy Henrietta's calculating eye.

Just before we left, a policeman came in, quite excited, and whispered something to Duncan. He was very obvious about it as he kept glancing in our direction all the time. For a moment I was not at all sure that Duncan would not change his mind and keep us there. He didn't, however. He sent us off with a renewed warning, to be within easy reach if he wanted us.

As I say, I was willing to forget the entire case and would have, had we not met Tweed as we left the building. There he stood grinning like the imp he was. "What gives?" he asked.

Henrietta was annoyed as she brushed past him but I knew that Mr. Tweed wouldn't brush off so easily. "I'll be with you in a moment," I promised. They walked on ahead to their waiting car. Peter roared off in his roadster while Tweed and I selected a spot out of earshot of the attendant policeman. A moment later a motorcycle roared by.

"What have you told your paper?" I demanded.

"Just that you were present at the investigation into the death of Martinique," he replied.

"No inference, no suggestions as to anyone's possible guilt?" I asked.

"I mentioned the names of the people Duncan was questioning, that's all."

"We have a secret, you and I, Tweed, which may lead to the real murderer. I haven't told Duncan about that bracelet."

"What's the dope on it?" he asked eagerly.

"I'm not going to tell you yet but I have a plan if you want to help. If you do, it might give you a beat on the story."

"But . . ." he began another protest.

"But me no buts," I snapped. "You either play ball with me or you don't. I can still go back and tell Duncan about the bracelet."

"Would you do that?" he asked, showing clearly that he did not think I would,

"I would. It might delay matters but that's his problem. I've had enough of it anyhow," I retorted.

"I guess you're on the level. Okay, I'll play ball. What do you want?" he asked.

"Run a story something like this, 'Inspector Duncan has released all suspects in the Martinique killing due to the unexpected discovery of a second murder by Officer Chitter, who found the body of Auriel Dodd in a secret room in the Martinique establishment.'"

"Wow" he cried. "You're not kidding?"

"No. That's the truth." I had to reach out and hold him, so anxious was he to dash off and telephone the news. "Just a moment. That isn't what I want. I'd like you to suggest that the missing Harold Dast is undoubtedly guilty of both crimes. No matter what else you say, be sure that is in the story," I cautioned.

"And what about the bracelet?" he asked.

"Put it in your office safe. Say nothing about it to anyone; promise me that." At his nod of agreement I said, "Run a personal, saying: 'Will trade bracelet for information.' I want you to get all answers to that personal. Keep me informed as to what happens."

"It's a deal," he agreed. "Is that all?"

"That's all."

"What do you expect to happen?"

"I'll tell you after the event," I said. "Now run along and get the presses going."

I was having my dinner in bed, dressed in a very gay and frilly gown of Stella's, when Peter finally arrived with my things. He was in a black mood when he stalked into the room and deposited my bags.

"Were you followed when you came here?" he demanded.

"You are imagining things," I said.

"Oh, no, I'm not. I was tailed by a motorcop from Martinique's to the hotel and from the hotel here. I tried to lose him but I wasn't smart enough," he said.

"That was a foolish thing to do," I said. "Why did you do it?"

"Because I don't like it."

"But you'll only make them more suspicious of you," I warned.

"This is probably what they want," he said and drew from his pocket an ugly-looking gun. He tossed it on the bed beside me.

"Take that thing away from me!" I cried. "I hate guns of any description."

He actually laughed at me, which did him a lot of good.

"Where did you get it?"

"It was in my car, and what is more it has been fired three times. What am I going to do with it?"

"Turn it over to Duncan," I said.

"And he'll think the birds dropped it in my car, I suppose," he snorted.

"He won't think much of you for trying to elude the men he has watching you."

"And I don't care what he thinks," Peter stormed. "That thing was a plant."

"And is now full of your fingerprints. Take this napkin and wipe it off. Leave it here with me. I'll turn it over to Duncan."

"Why is he tailing me?" Peter demanded.

"Because you showed interest in the French girl; because you admit you went back to that apartment this afternoon; because he has the picture taken by Martinique the night Dast is supposed to have died," I explained.

"Why doesn't he look for Dast?" he exclaimed.

"He's doing that right now."

"But he'd rather think I did it," he grumbled.

"You need some dinner and rest, Peter. Why don't you get both," I suggested. "And, Peter," I warned as he left with Stella, "don't do anything foolish for a day or two."

As Henrietta helped to tuck me in for the night she said, "I wasn't very gracious this afternoon, Ethel. I'm sorry. I was frightfully upset, as you can imagine. I don't know all that you have done but I feel quite confident that whatever it was, it kept Stella and that young man out of jail. I am truly grateful."

"You'd better make up your mind, Henrietta, that that young man is going to be your son-in-law. If you get used to the idea it might make things easier for Stella when it happens."

"This Hollywood has made changes in my life," she sighed. "Would you believe it, Ethel, that I have reached a point where some things don't seem to matter any more?"

"You're growing up," I said. "Your sense of proportion has changed. It's a sign, too, that you're growing older and you can thank God that you are doing it gracefully."

"I've always tried to do the right thing," she said.

"Fiddlesticks," I retorted. "The right thing is the warm human thing. You're tired and upset. Don't worry any more about it tonight." I patted the hand which still rested on the coverlet. She actually held my arm for a moment, then left me.

My tired muscles soothed by a warm bath, a few of my own things about me, I felt as contented as a cat, stretched and went to sleep immediately.

It was bright and sunny when I awoke and rang for my coffee. Stella had been waiting for me. She came in with the morning papers. Tweed had kept his word. The story as I wanted it had a prominent place on the front page.

The other papers ran large heads too, announcing that: HAROLD DAST HOLLYWOOD EXTRA WANTED BY POLICE FOR MARTINIQUE MURDER.

Tweed's paper was the only one that had carried the report of the double murder.

"What's going to happen?" Stella asked as I dropped the papers after that first quick look.

Before I could answer a maid came in with a tray and the telephone which she plugged in at the head of my bed. "A Mr. Tweed is on the wire. Will you talk to him?" she asked.

Tweed was breathless. "The cops have been on my tail about the Dodd killing. Duncan tried to make me admit that you gave me the dope, but I kept mum. Hear from him yet?"

"No. I just woke up," I replied.

"What's on your mind? What do you expect to happen?" he asked with that same breathless eagerness so typical of him. "Can't you tell a fellow?"

"Not now. You'll have to be patient."

"I could tell the cops what I know about you," he teased.

"Go ahead and see what it gets you," I retorted. "Any bites from the personal ad?"

"No. How are you feeling this morning?"

"Fine. I had a good sleep. Did you put the bracelet away safely?"

"Yeah. Why is it so important?" he coaxed.

"Later, if you're a good boy, I'll tell you," I replied.

"Do you want me to give out your address?" he asked.

"You've done that already. Why on earth did you tell the world I came here?" I demanded, recalling his account of my transfer from the hotel.

"Because you're good copy," he answered.

"Don't do it again," I warned.

"Okay, toots," he replied and rang off.

"Toots to you," I said with a smile as I replaced the receiver.

A moment later the telephone rang again. It was a strange voice which asked for me. When I assured the speaker of my identity it said: "I want that bracelet. If you value your life, you'll turn it over to me."

"How?" I asked.

"Have it with you the next time we meet. I'll arrange the meeting and no monkey business, remember!"

"I'm not leaving this house. If you want it, you'll have to come here. The police will know nothing about it," I added.

I waited for an answer but he did not speak. After a moment, the line went dead. It was a man's voice. My suspicions were taking concrete form at last. I felt pleased.

Stella had been pacing up and down before the windows.

"What is it?" I demanded. "Why are you so restless?"

"I'm worried about Peter."

"Why?"

"He's so foolhardy. I had a frightful time with him last night. He wanted to go out and ride about the city in an attempt to elude the police. After much argument, Mother's included, he finally consented to stay here."

"Where is he now?"

"Sleeping. How can he sleep when none of us know what is going to happen to us?"

"Men are like that. He'll wake up, have a shower, eat a good breakfast and then barge in here full of ideas. Don't fuss about him."

"But, Ethel, we're not through with this yet. You and Peter were in Dast's apartment yesterday."

"I don't believe Duncan suspects us of her death now," I assured her.

"I'm not thinking of Duncan. I'm thinking of the danger to you and Peter."

"Danger?"

"Yes. If I were the murderer I would be worried about both of you, what you saw, what you might remember that would mean my conviction."

"Fiddlesticks, my dear. There is nothing to worry about on that score."

"I wish I had your optimism."

"You will when you reach my age. Put all such ideas out of your pretty head. Why don't you go and rouse Peter. He'd probably like being awakened by you. Men are funny creatures when they're in love. He'd adore you today for wakening him, but once you are married, let him sleep as long as he likes."

She took to the idea and was on the point of leaving when a maid came to say that a woman who would give no name was asking to see me. "She says it's very important. She seems nervous-like, jumpy if you know what I mean," she explained.

"Young or old?" I asked, hoping that it might prove to be Alice French.

"She's not so young, but I don't know, sort of tall," the maid explained.

Then it was not Alice French. My curiosity was aroused.

"Show her up," I ordered. "You'd better leave me alone with her," I suggested to Stella. She straightened the bedclothes, gave me an affectionate pat on the cheek and left.

The woman came in, hesitantly following the maid.

"I'm Mrs. Dast," she said when we were alone. She was expensively dressed in a dark, tight-fitting gown under a drum-major's cape. She was more than average height and wore a ridiculous hat perched over one eye. Her hair was bleached. Her feet were rather too large but tastefully shod. It was a good ensemble. Her mouth was too red, as were the nails on her long tapering fingers. She carried a handsome black handbag which she held in front of her. I would have been fooled completely if I had not had reason to suspect the identity of my caller.

"Mrs. Dast," I repeated the name. "You don't mean that you are the mother of the young man. . ."

She nodded. "I would like you to help my son. The police are after him."

"So I see by the papers. What do you think I could do?" I asked.

"You are versed in crime. You . . ." She opened her bag and took out a dainty handkerchief which she put to her nose. Her voice was pleasantly husky.

"You overestimate my ability," I said.

"Not for a moment." There was a complete change of tone. It was a man's voice that spoke those words. Cleverly, like a magician, he had distracted my attention. While I had been watching the hand with the handkerchief his other hand had produced a revolver from the purse. Gone were all the little feminine traits that had been so convincing when he came in. "You know what I want," he said, as I gazed fascinated into the barrel of his revolver.

CHAPTER FOURTEEN

I CAN NEVER FACE a gun without some nervous fear crawling up and down my spine. True, that same hand had threatened me with a gun once before, had terrified me to a point of desperation, but the finger had not pressed the trigger, would not press it now, of that I was sure as I gazed into his eyes.

"Put up that silly gun, Harold!" I said familiarly, hoping it would work. I saw the directness of his gaze waver. "You know I'm not afraid of you," I managed to say with more sureness. "Come over here and sit down. I want to talk to you."

"I don't want to talk to you. I want the bracelet." He advanced slowly, threateningly. "You said there would be no police here. You lied," he accused. "If I have to shoot my way out, I'll kill you first."

I laughed. He was so tense, so dramatic, so much the cornered desperado.

"Come on! I'm desperate," he said. "I don't want to hurt you," he added nervously.

If I had had the bracelet with me I think I would have given it to him. As he drew closer I could see how harried his eyes were, how red from lack of sleep, how drawn his face under the heavy makeup.

"You should have thought of that when you cracked me over the head," I said. "See." I was going to show him the lump which was still egg-size and painful at the edge of my transformation.

"Keep your hands down!" he snapped.

"Very well. Now sit down! You don't suppose I'd be fool enough to have the bracelet here, do you?" I asked.

"I don't know what you will do."

"Sit down," I repeated irritably. "You make me nervous; that thing might go off and then we'd both be in a mess. Now, forget the police if you can; they are watching Peter Bradley, who stayed here overnight."

"They saw me come in. If this is a trap . . ."

"It's not a trap. No one knows about your disguise but me."

"Are you telling me the truth?"

"Yes."

"How did you know?" he asked anxiously.

"I figured the thing out. When I discovered that you were not dead, the pieces fitted together into a reasonable whole. I hoped you would come to me as soon as you knew where I was. You did not disappoint me."

"What made you so sure I would come?" he demanded.

"I know how desperate you must be. I have your bracelet—but not here," I added quickly. "You have some information that I want, also my four thousand dollars. Did you kill Martinique?"

"No. I wish I had."

"You may be very glad that you did not. Did you kill Auriel Dodd?"

"No. Who did?" he demanded.

"I don't know. I had hoped you might give me some clew."

"I thought it was Martinique," he said.

"Martinique died first, died too soon, because my grandniece Stella Wayne and Peter Bradley are still under suspicion. Duncan found the picture Martinique took that night in your apartment. It is a bad bit of evidence against them. That is why I wanted to talk to you."

"I can't give myself up. Haven't you read the papers?" he cried. "They are hunting for me."

"Where will you go?" I demanded.

"I don't know," he said in despair. "I can't do this much longer." He indicated his feminine clothes. "I'll make a slip and that will be the end of me."

"You'd better do business with me," I suggested.

"Have I any choice?" he asked hopelessly.

"You can walk out of here if you choose to do so. Do you want to do that?"

"No. I don't know what I want to do. I want to be free."

"Why did you assume the masquerade?"

"Martinique made me do it. I've done it before. He wanted Bradley to think he had killed me. I was to be a girl for a few days and then he said I could come back. Things have gone all wrong. Even Alice came back from New York unexpectedly."

"Didn't you send for her?" I asked. "I think she thought you had."

"I know. She received a telegram—she thought it was from me—it was signed with my name. That's one of the things I can't understand, Miss Thomas. Martinique sent her to New York with a lot of money."

"Money?" I repeated.

"Yes. I think he planned to get away—why, I don't know. When Alice received the telegram she thought I had found out about the money and wanted to steal it."

"And she brought it back with her?" I asked.

"Yes."

"She loves you very much."

"I realize that now. I want to be worthy of it." He said it so simply that I believed him.

"Where is she now?"

"I won't tell you that. I want her to be safe, no matter what becomes of me."

"She has the money."

"No. It is gone. She left it at the apartment."

"A nasty habit she has, leaving things," I remarked tersely. "She left me in that bed-closet."

"She was sorry about that. She didn't know what to do. She hoped Auriel would go away. She waited outside for a long time. When she finally went back she said there was talk and commotion in the hall. She didn't want to be seen, so she slipped away."

"What happened to the money?"

"We don't know. It was gone when I went back there."

"And while we are on the subject, what happened to her at the hotel? She vanished into thin air."

"That was my fault. I found Auriel's body. I knew Alice had been there, had talked to Auriel. I was afraid she would be implicated. I made her hide."

"With the money gone you were on a spot," I agreed. "Any ideas about the murders?"

"If you or Bradley didn't kill them . . ."

"Don't talk rubbish. You know very well I had nothing to do with them, nor did Peter."

"All right, all right," he tried to appease my indignation. "Then my guess is either Enrico or Alvera."

"Why?"

"Because they are the only ones who could have all the information."

"That's a point," I admitted. "Now, tell me something else. What hold did Martinique have over you?"

"The bracelets. They belonged to my mother. Sometime ago while she was away I ran out of money. I took the bracelets and some other jewelry and pawned them. When I did get some extra money I redeemed them. I was going to put them back, but I was too late. My mother had returned from her trip unexpectedly and had reported the theft. Instead of making a clean breast of it then, I hid them. A day or two later, Martinique looked me up. He knew all about the bracelets and their reported theft. He must have learned about them from the pawnbroker. He threatened to expose me unless I did a little job for him. I know I was a fool to have done it but I felt helpless. Don't you see what would have happened to me if the story were made public? It would have stamped me as a thief as well as well, no one would ever believe that I dress like this because I have to; they'd think I do it because I am queer and want to do it."

"Just what did you do for Martinique?"

"I got men and women into compromising situations for him. He was a blackmailer de luxe."

"There were always pictures?" I asked.

He had the grace to blush. "Yes."

"What do you know about Tim Flannigan?"

"Martinique has been getting to him for years. Every time Flannigan got a good client, Martinique took him."

"But Martinique wasn't an agent, was he?"

"Not exactly. He said he managed people. He ran Hollywood."

"How?" I asked.

"By fear."

"Would Flannigan be familiar with Martinique's establishment, the building, the passageways?"

"He would know most of them, yes."

"Did he know Alice French?"

"She was a client of his when she was out here before. She left him for Martinique."

"What about this time? I understand she has been away from Hollywood until recently?"

"Same old story. Flannigan handled her while she was staging her comeback, doing personal appearances and that sort of thing. When she arrived in Hollywood, Martinique grabbed her again. You mustn't blame her," he said. "Martinique never gave a person a chance. Flannigan was awful sore but she couldn't help herself."

"How about Auriel Dodd, your ex-wife?"

"Same thing. How did you know I had been married to her?"

I laughed. It was such an incongruous question coming from him made up so meticulously to look like a smart modern woman.

"I had you looked up in New York. I have a friend there connected with the police. It was his report that gave me the first clew to your disguise. Then I found some of your clothes in the closet."

"What's going to happen to me, Miss Thomas?"

"That I don't know. I had hoped you might be able to give me some clew to work on. Duncan is inclined to think you guilty."

"And what do you think?"

I studied him carefully for a moment, trying to see the man under the makeup. His eyes were less harried than they had been on his entrance. They were rather large, round and full, with liquid brown centers that might be rather appealing. There were shadows under them, not quite bags but the first indications of over-indulgence and excess. His nose was straight and slightly pointed over a pleasantly weak mouth. The lips were full, not quite sensuous but certainly not strong. His chin was softly rounded and dimpled. When he smiled there were dimples in his cheeks. The man I tried to see was generally considered good-looking but not strong. You would say, "Isn't he good-looking!" if you were a woman of discernment but never, "What a handsome man!"

"You are making me very uncomfortable," he said uneasily, squirming under my scrutiny.

"I don't know what to think about you. At first I thought you must be guilty," I said honestly. "My introduction to you through Stella and Peter was not too good. Alice French made me feel that there must be something decent about you to warrant the love you had inspired. After that you hit me over the head. Then, not satisfied with that, you threatened to kill me at Martinique's and came in here with the same threat in your mind." He had been looking at the floor as I started to talk. As I went on he had the courage to lift his head and look me squarely in the eyes. "You are not a strong man, you have been easily led and influenced, but that is not entirely your fault. You have had a handicap to overcome." At his surprise I said, "Too much mother."

"You don't know how true that is," he agreed.

"Don't make excuses for yourself because of it," I cautioned.

He flushed under his makeup. "I wasn't really," he mumbled in self-justification.

"Did you kill Auriel Dodd?" I shot the question at him unexpectedly.

"Good God, no!"

"Then you didn't kill Martinique?"

"No. I meant to. I went to his office through the passageway to do it. He wasn't there. The room was empty. Just as I was about to step out Enrico came into the office. I didn't want him to see me because I was waiting for Martinique. I wanted him to die."

"Enrico came into the room, you say?" I asked eagerly.

"Yes. He looked about. Just at that moment, someone below tried to get the lift in which I was standing. I stepped back into the secret corridor and allowed the lift to go down."

"Were you in the lift when you tried to force me to give up the bracelet?"

"Not at first. I moved into it. There is an opening in the grille so that one can look into the office."

"To get back to Enrico. What did he do when he entered the room?"

"Nothing. He closed the door rather carefully, looked about, then crossed to the lift. He went down in the car just after Auriel stepped into the room."

"Auriel Dodd? How did he do that?"

"He went into the hall. When she stepped into the office, he entered the lift from the hall. It has three doors."

"Did Auriel see him?"

"No."

"Too bad. It might have been the clew we needed."

"She couldn't have seen him."

"Did you stand behind that wall all through the police investigation?" I asked, amazed.

"Yes. I wanted to be sure of you."

"Tell me something else. Did you see Peter and Stella when they were in the room?"

"I didn't see them enter. I wasn't looking either time. I heard a noise and looked out and there they were."

"But you know they are innocent."

"I didn't see them kill him."

"Did you know he was dead until I opened the door and his body fell out?"

"No. You certainly were a cool one, but you couldn't get away with it, could you? I'm surprised no one saw you."

I had been thinking about all he had said. He had given an alibi to everyone with the exception of Henrietta, Flannigan and Miss Alvera. I couldn't believe that Flannigan had killed Auriel Dodd because of the voice I had heard. If Flannigan killed Martinique there was no connection between the two murders. The same thing was true of Henrietta. She admitted she was willing, anxious, to kill the man but her ardor grew cold while she waited for Flannigan to come out. She was undoubtedly saved by her kidneys. That then left only one person who might have killed them both—Miss Alvera.

"What about Miss Alvera? Just what was her position there?" I asked.

"She was really the second in command, a partner of his."

"Really?" I've no idea why I doubted his statement. I didn't mean to.

"She's the only one who knew as much about his business as he did," he stated emphatically to overcome my expressed doubt.

"Could you imagine her killing Auriel Dodd?" I asked.

"I could imagine her doing anything. She's made of iron, that woman, and completely corroded. Her shell is all rust," he said bitterly.

"Would she kill them both?" I went on.

"For a good reason, yes."

"Would Martinique's proposed trip have anything to do with it?" I asked.

"It might," he conceded.

"He was going away, flying to New York on tonight's plane," I said.

"Not Martinique," he stated definitely. "He was afraid of planes."

"But he had a ticket. He was going. Duncan believes he was clearing out for good."

"Not Martinique, not by plane," he insisted. "The murderer perhaps, but not Martinique."

"Remember your positive conviction on that point."

"Why?"

"I want you ready to talk when the time comes," I warned him.

"And take the rap for assaulting an officer?" he asked.

"That may not be necessary. You and I are the only ones who know about that. It can be one of the mysterious angles of the case. We don't have to clean everything up, do we?" I asked.

"If you say we don't, we don't," he agreed. "Do you want me to give myself up right away?" he asked willingly.

"I don't think so. While the hue and cry is on for you, the murderer is going to feel safe and perhaps bold. What were your plans before you came here?"

"I didn't have any really. I was going to hang around and live on your four thousand. There's no place for me to go."

"Although the police are looking for you they haven't penetrated your disguise yet. Duncan may figure it out."

"He probably will," he said hopelessly.

"You'd better go," I said, as I glanced at the clock.

"All right. I'll keep in touch with you," he promised.

I had an idea. The poor lad was a pathetic figure as he went to the mirror and touched up his disguise. "Do you want to feel safe for a few days?" I asked.

"And how!" he said.

"Fine. For the next few days you can pose as my companion. I'll arrange for a room for you at the hotel." I called while he waited and told the clerk to have a room prepared for my companion, that she would arrive shortly.

"Your name will be Helen Conklin. Don't forget. Go up there and wait until you hear from me. Better have your meals in the room. I'll have the bracelet for you too," I promised.

"Thank you," he said simply and without affectation.

I watched him go. He had all the makings of a rogue. He had probably done a great many things that would not bear too close investigation. He had stolen my four thousand dollars, had attacked an officer of the law, had been a part of Martinique's nefarious schemes; he was a hunted man but a sorrowful one. I felt sorry for him. Left to himself he might go from bad to worse. No point in making a hardened criminal out of him. I hoped he had learned his lesson. The girl might keep him straight. I hoped so.

I had done my one good deed for the day. I should have been satisfied. I should have waited patiently for Duncan to do the rest. But I did nothing of the kind. As I lay there, I began putting two and two together. I wanted to know more about Martinique's business. I was fool enough to think that I could solve the case faster than the Los Angeles police. With my mind made up for action, I began to dress.

A maid came to inform me that Chitter wanted to see me. "He's downstairs waiting," she said. There was something about the quickness of her breath that made me think Chitter had made a conquest. He could go to the head of many women, that handsome giant.

"Handsome, isn't he?" I asked her.

"Yes, ma'am," she agreed, blushing prettily.

"What the devil does he want?" I grumbled.

"He didn't say, ma'am."

"Show him up."

He came in, resplendent in his uniform. He was shy. He twirled his cap in his hand.

"Well, Chitter," I greeted. "Come in. Sit down; you look tired."

"I am. I've had no sleep."

"What kept you up all night?" I asked.

"Work."

"Did you find something?"

"It's because I didn't find it," he replied gloomily. "I'm in bad with Duncan." He twirled his cap.

"Maybe I can square you with him," I suggested.

"That ain't why I came," he answered artlessly.

"I been thinking about us, you and me, and the crack I got on the head."

"What about mine? Two heads are better than one."

"That's it. That's what I mean. Why were you searched and I wasn't? That's what's bothering me. This Dast fellow they're looking for, maybe it was him in there that hit us."

"What makes you think that?"

"Well, it was an awful wallop I got."

"Mine too," I replied.

"Now, what would he think you'd have that I didn't?" He went back to his point with dogged determination. "He didn't search me," he stated bluntly.

"Perhaps there wasn't time," I suggested. "I rather covered you up, you know. I fell on top of you."

"I think you're keeping something back, Miss Thomas. I'm sure you had something he wanted."

"I had four thousand dollars which I lost. That must have been it. Whoever it was must have known I had the money on me."

"I still have a hunch that it was more than that. Did you pick anything up while you were in that room when the Dodd girl was killed?"

"Only the wad which I gave to Duncan," I replied.

"It beats me," he said puzzled. "I know I'm right though, Miss Thomas. It must be the Dast fellow. He was probably hiding there all the time and heard you. He needed the money to get away. I'd like to break this case. I'll get a promotion if I do. It's got to be Dast."

"It doesn't have to be anyone but the right man," I said. "Dast did not do it."

"Then who did?" he demanded. "You know you won't admit Bradley had anything to do with it in spite of everything."

"Don't be silly, Chitter."

"It ain't silly. While you and I were looking around yesterday afternoon the others weren't watched very carefully. Duncan was busy going over prints and things with the men. They were not allowed to leave the building but they did roam around. How do we know? There may be another corridor like the one we found."

"Did you find any?"

"No, ma'am."

"And what does it have to do with Peter Bradley and his possible guilt?" I demanded.

"Why did he disappear?" he asked.

"He what?" I fairly shouted at him.

"I lost him last night. That's why I'm in bad with Duncan."

"He didn't disappear. He spent the night here. He's probably eating his breakfast right now," I said.

"They told me he slipped out the back way," he said, "and I believed them. Well, Duncan wants you and Bradley; he's investigating Auriel Dodd's death."

"What about the gun in Peter's car?" I demanded.

"Well, it was like this. One of the men found the gun in Bradley's car. It had been fired three times. He came back and told Duncan just when you were leaving."

"It was a plant," I said, trying to dismiss it.

"I don't know nothing about that. Duncan told me to trail Bradley to see if he would do anything about the gun. You know, try to get rid of it."

"Wait a minute. Why didn't the officer take the gun to Duncan?"

"Duncan works different than a lot of men. If we find evidence we never touch it or take it away. We leave it and report to him. He has an idea that if you give a suspected man enough rope he will hang himself. That's why the gun was left in Bradley's car. I followed him to the hotel and then trailed him here last night. What did he do with the gun, Miss Thomas?"

"I have it. I'll bring it with us."

I went to the cupboard for a wrap and saw the wreck of the gown I had been wearing. It had been ripped and torn when Harold searched me. Suddenly the stain on the sleeve became significant. Of course! There could be no other explanation! It was brownish and looked as if I had encountered some dark paint somewhere.

I rolled the dress into a ball and handed it to Chitter. "Take this to someone who can tell you whether or not that stain is blood," I ordered. "Then meet me at Martinique's. I'll have Bradley with me."

CHAPTER FIFTEEN

PETER DROVE ME to Martinique's. How different this ride was from the one taken yesterday! Then I had been ridden by fear, for I had just heard Peter's explosive threat to kill a man. That man had died, a girl had died, and I had been drifting in a fog. There had been things I had wanted to see and things that I had purposely avoided. I had wanted to believe in Harold Dast's innocence and yet there was a doubt in my mind since I had thought about that stain on my bodice. I had noticed it first after my escape from the apartment. At that time I had assumed that it had come from the pole to which I had clung. Perhaps it did. But suppose it was blood? If it was it shattered a growing conviction, one to which I wanted to hold. In the light of the things Dast had told me my theory could not be true.

If Dast spoke the truth and saw Enrico enter Martinique's office and then leave via the elevator just after Auriel Dodd stepped into the room, Enrico was not the murderer. Except for that statement of Dast's Enrico had to be the criminal. He had opportunity. He was furious at Martinique. He didn't know Alice French had arrived on the plane, however, but he knew about it later that day. In like manner Dast furnished Peter, Stella, Alice French and myself with alibis. Martinique had been murdered and his body put into the closet before our separate arrivals at the room. That left Miss Alvera, Henrietta and Flannigan.

I would tell Duncan and let him decide which of the three was guilty. I felt a little uneasy about Henrietta. Had that melting of her icy shell been brought about by an act of violence? How horrible it would be for Stella if that were true. I must have shuddered at the prospect, for Peter asked, "Cold?"

"No. Just bewildered. I was considering the possibility of Henrietta's guilt."

"Ridiculous!" he snapped.

"The case has narrowed down to three people."

"But not Mrs. Wayne. She couldn't have done it."

"She has no alibi for herself. She might have followed Auriel Dodd. We none of us know what happened before that girl died."

"I still say, rubbish."

I was not to be denied my gloomy thoughts, however. "If she is guilty no jury in the world will convict her when the facts become known. What a case it will be!"

"Have you gone mad?" he demanded.

"No, not quite."

"Who are the remaining prime suspects?" he asked.

"Flannigan and Miss Alvera. No one actually saw Martinique after Flannigan went into his office. If Flannigan killed him he put him into the closet and walked out, bold as brass. Flannigan lived in the apartment. Flannigan was afraid of Martinique. Flannigan was furious. I egged him on."

"Flannigan might answer the requirements," Peter agreed. "Who is the other one?"

"Miss Alvera."

"But why should she?"

"I don't know. I know nothing about the woman except an instinctive dislike which I felt immediately. Peter! Suppose she was in love with him. Suppose she knew he had been planning to leave and wanted to go with him."

"And he refused to take her," Peter suggested, "and so like a woman scorned she killed him. Is that what you mean?"

"Something like that, yes."

"What makes you so sure that there are no other suspects?"

I told him then that I had located Harold Dast, told him about the passage through the elevator, and the things that Dast had seen that afternoon.

"All of which can be lies," he said. "Dast is a weak sister or he would never have been a part of anything as rotten as Martinique."

"We're not all strong, Peter," I reminded him. "Martinique planned to use you. That's why he went to the trouble of frightening you the way he did."

"And what would have become of Dast?" Peter demanded.

That question was a poser and one that needed careful thought. Suppose Martinique had planned to do away with Dast and in that way always keep his hold over Stella and Peter. It was not unlikely. Perhaps that was how he had gained such a hold over countless men and women, so that they would do his bidding— Flannigan, Dast and others. If Dast knew that, then he would have wanted Martinique dead and out of the way.

"It's too much for me at the moment, Peter."

There was a policeman on guard at Martinique's keeping the curious away from the entrance. I have since learned that Los Angeles people are the greatest lookers in the world. I know that an account in the paper of an unusual event brings them out by the thousands. A heavy tide and some beach damage, the ignition of an oil well, a premiere, an opening night at the theatre, is incentive enough to bring droves of people to clutter the highways.

"The morbid and the curious are here," he said as we were waved beyond the entrance.

"I'll walk back with you," I said quickly.

When he found a place to park I went to that pole I had embraced. It was dry, round and smooth.

There was a gleam in Peter's eye as he watched me. "Am I supposed to ask what the pole has to do with the case?"

"No. I don't know myself. There was a time when I believed it important."

"Stella is worried about us. She cautioned me to be careful, to take care of you. She has been reading too many detective yarns and has reached the point where she expects not only a second but a third murder."

"So she told me. It will do us no harm to be careful."

The officer on duty did not want to pass us into the building. I was arguing with him when Chitter zoomed up on his motorcycle, glowered at Peter and then took us in. "I'll have a report on that dress in a little while," he said.

When I faced Duncan in the foyer where he was superintending an examination of Martinique's records I handed him the bundle in which the gun was wrapped and said, "Here's your gun, and Bradley. I should think you'd have had sense enough to know it was a plant."

"I did," he said, "but I didn't want anyone to know I knew it. You rather spoiled my plan by bringing it back."

"Who owned it?" I demanded.

"Martinique," he replied. "My man had taken the number. We traced it."

"Peter gave it to me last night. You might have saved yourself some trouble."

"No trouble at all. Glad to know Bradley didn't try to get rid of it. I felt hopeful about him when he tried to elude my man early in the evening."

"He just didn't like the idea of being followed," I snapped.

Duncan winked at Peter. "Mind waiting? I'll be ready for you both in a few minutes."

"What on earth are you doing there?" I asked, pointing at the files scattered about.

"Going over Martinique's records," he replied. "Ingenious, wasn't it?"

It certainly was. The entire wall behind Miss Alvera's desk in the foyer was a honeycomb of hidden filing cases. Each square panel was a door that opened into a space large enough to slide a drawer from an ordinary filing cabinet.

I walked past the desk and peered into the office from which Enrico said he had seen me through wall mirrors. I looked up. The man had been right. By looking into those mirrors a person could see the entire gallery.

Duncan had followed us in. "Have you found anything in those records?" I asked.

"Enough to blast the city of Los Angeles, or should I say Hollywood?" he replied.

"Pictures?"

"Pictures," he repeated. "They would make those postcards from Paris blush, some of them."

"May I see them?" I asked boldly.

"You ought to be ashamed of yourself, an old woman like you," he chided. "No one will see them. When the case is finished they will be destroyed, and when they are, a lot of people will sleep easier."

"A perfect blackmail setup, eh?"

"It looks that way. Have fun," he teased, turning away.

Duncan and his men were very busy, too busy to worry about us. I poked about here and there looking into things. I chanced upon bits of conversation, heard names read off as they went through the files. What a man Martinique had been, what a loathsome business he had conducted! No wonder he had died; the great wonder was that he had been allowed to live so long.

I became restless. Peter certainly did not enjoy trailing me about and yet I knew he was following Stella's instructions, protecting me, but from what?

With Henrietta in mind as a possible suspect I decided to go to the powder room. As I started away Peter followed. "Can't I go to the powder room alone?" I demanded.

He smiled, bowed and turned away.

The door to the powder room was in the back hall close to the entrance of the lift. A person could very easily, if they knew the mechanics of the automatic elevator, slip through it into Martinique's office. As I turned away I saw Flannigan coming up the stairs from the room below. I was surprised and it must have shown on my face, because he explained that Duncan had called him and being lazy he had come by the shortcut.

"Duncan's finding all sorts of things back there," I said, pointing to the mass of papers being taken from the files.

Flannigan's face clouded for a moment, then he shrugged. "It can't be helped," he said. "I hope there are no blackmailers in Duncan's outfit."

"From what he just said, some of it must be pretty bad."

"If you weren't a woman I could tell you a few things," he said with full male superiority.

"I know my A B C's," I replied hopefully.

I enjoy a bit of scandal as well as the next person. What normal woman doesn't? I never repeat malicious gossip, but Flannigan didn't give me a chance.

"There are some things a man doesn't discuss with . . ." he paused and then continued, "with his clients." His face broke into a genial smile.

It was difficult for me to believe that Flannigan, no matter what hold Martinique had had over him, could be the murderer.

"Why did you let yourself get into his power?" I demanded.

"It wasn't a thing you set out to do," he replied thoughtfully. "He knew a lot of tricks. He understood human weakness better than most people. He was always ready to take the advantage. Some people he gripped through money, the gambling, others he caught with other bait."

"Men and women," I suggested.

There was embarrassed panic in his eyes. He nodded and passed on.

I followed him as he reported to Duncan. I heard Duncan say, "I won't be ready for you for ten or fifteen minutes. Your apartment is two-fifty, isn't it?"

Flannigan nodded.

Duncan had glanced down at a sheet of paper on the desk in front of him. I moved to his side and with pretended indifference looked at that paper. The names of the people connected with the murder were listed. Martinique, Miss Alvera, Dast, Flannigan, Alice French and Enrico all lived in the apartment next door. Opposite their names I found the numbers of their apartments.

Duncan realized what I was doing and said, "I wouldn't try anything on my own if I were you."

I should have recognized the remark for the warning that it was, but being a determined, foolhardy old woman with ideas of my own I moved away, nodded to Peter, and led him into Martinique's office.

"Now what?" he asked.

"A little experiment. I need your help. Close the door."

I saw Chitter's anxious eyes on us as the door closed.

"Unless you know what you're doing, an experiment might be risky," Peter warned.

I was fed up with warnings, fed up with Duncan taking time to plow through all those records when the solution of the murder should be under way. Those of us who do not understand police methods are apt to be too critical. The police work is hard, monotonous, painstaking but thorough. Police detection is diligence first, followed by brilliant deduction.

I had opened the door of the lift and was ready to step inside.

"I'm going inside. Go to the door and walk toward the desk. I'll tell you when to stop." Peter's eyes were rebellious, doubtful as I allowed the door to slide shut.

Dast had told me that he had been in the lift or in the corridor just behind the third panel of the lift. The plan of the floor was clearly in my mind as I stepped into the corridor and found the hole in the grill through which Harold Dast had watched. I felt confident that the secret corridor had been designed originally as a convenient means of egress to and from the two buildings.

I could not see Peter at all. I asked him to walk forward toward the desk. It was then that I realized that Dast's statement to me did not give any of us an alibi. From the peephole it was impossible to see a person entering the room from the main hall. That was what I wanted to know.

"All right, Peter," I called.

There was one other point I wanted to settle. I was looking for another door—a direct entrance to the building from Martinique's office—an easier way than the one through Dast's apartment.

"What are you doing?" Peter demanded.

"Thinking," I replied as I fingered the walls. "I'll be out in a minute."

I found it. Directly opposite the entrance to the lift there was another door which Chitter and I had missed the day before.

"Can't you think out here?" I heard Peter ask as I cautiously opened this door and realized I was in the main hall of the apartment building, the third-floor hall.

That discovery was satisfying. I knew then that I was right. I needed some evidence, however, to substantiate my theory. I was probably too late, but one never knows when dealing with criminals just how their minds work. It was a chance I felt I must take.

The corridor seemed so innocent today. There was none of the dread that I had felt when I had been there before. There were no excited voices on the floor below. Ahead of me I could see the entrance to Dast's apartment but I was no longer interested in that. I was trying to remember the list of names and numbers I had seen on the desk in front of Duncan just a few minutes before.

If I had had the sense of a nitwit I would have gone back to Duncan and told him, but I didn't. I forged ahead, fed by my vanity and my desire to end the case. I don't know why I even expected doors to be unlocked, nor do I know why the one door I wanted to find should have been open. Perhaps it is true that a protecting Providence watches over fools. The door was open, the latch had not caught. I went in and in a closet found the one bit of evidence I had wanted. I could not believe my luck. I slipped across the room to the telephone, eager now to tell Duncan of my discovery. Just as I lifted the receiver a voice warned harshly, "I wouldn't do that if I were you."

The implement slipped from my paralyzed fingers and clattered back into position. I was paralyzed with fear. I knew I was totally at the mercy of the killer. There was no need to turn and look. I had no desire to face death, for I knew it waited for me. I found myself wondering why the man didn't shoot and have done with it. It's come at last, I told myself. And then I felt strangely philosophical, thinking that I had lived a long time, had had a full and abundant life.

The delay was irksome. One cannot stand on the brink of the Great Divide waiting forever for the blow to strike. My voice was constricted, did not sound at all like mine, as I managed to say, "My death will do you no good. You will be caught."

"Your precious friend Bradley will hang for it," he said. "He was last seen with you."

That statement was true. I knew it. Peter would undoubtedly be arrested. It might be a long time before they were able to put the pieces of the puzzle together. What a conceited fool I had been.

Then the shot came. It tore past my head and ripped into the wall. I swirled around and saw Peter struggling with the man, fighting desperately to get the gun, struggling as he must have struggled that night with Harold Dast. Only this time it was not a plot staged to fool Peter. It was a desperate struggle for his life and mine.

I backed to the wall, out of the way, as they fought and tumbled, rolling over and over, growling, groaning, straining, each of them fighting for life. In such melodramatic circumstances there should have been something for me to do, some opportunity to help Peter.

To my everlasting shame, several seconds elapsed before
I realized that the phone was right there in front of me.
But as I reached for it I knew also, and with certainty,
that no call for the police could bring help in time; and as
I lifted the mouth-and-ear piece, the tossing, heaving
bodies lunged against the desk. I heard cloth rip. Peter
staggered, was on his knees, trying to rise, his back
toward me. The killer's bleeding face, his hot breath, then
his hair and shoulders, came between me and Peter. For
the fraction of a moment opportunity came, and I took it.

I felt the weight of the receiver in my hand; with all
the strength I could muster I struck at that loathsome
head, just behind the ear, at the base of the skull. I felt
rather than heard the thud of the blow. There was a
groan, more of grunt, and the man's fingers slithered
away from the tearing grasp they had on Peter's face. It
was a feeling of jubilant relief which preceded my
completely feminine reaction. For one of the few times in
my life I fainted.

CHAPTER SIXTEEN

PETER WAS BENDING over me anxiously when I opened my eyes. The carnage was over; Peter and I were alone.

"How long have I been like this?" I managed to ask.

"A few minutes."

"You saved my life, Peter."

"You solved the riddle," he countered. "Where is he?"

"He was taken to Martinique's office with the others. Duncan was pretty sore at what happened."

"What did he say?"

"'Deliver me from women detectives!' or something like that."

"He's right, Peter. I think this is my last murder."

"If your friends keep out of trouble it might be," he said. "You're like an old fire-horse, you know. You're swell," he added.

I love a sincere compliment. I know I glowed as I pulled myself together. "I might as well face the music," I said, getting up.

"There's no hurry now," he advised.

My hand was shaking as I picked up the phone mouthpiece, that had dropped to the floor. I called my hotel and asked for Helen Conklin. When Harold answered I asked quickly, "Is that you, Helen?"

I sensed the relief in his voice, the relaxation of his throat muscles, as he said, "I didn't know whether to answer or not. Anything happen?"

"Come to Martinique's at once. Bring Alice French with you if possible. Hurry! It is all over."

"Are you sure?"

"Come at once!" I rang off to prevent further discussion.

"Now, who is Helen Conklin?" Peter asked.

I told him then about Harold, how Martinique had used Harold's past as a female impersonator to further his own ends.

"Well, I'll be darned!" Peter exclaimed, which I understand is the normal man's reaction to female impersonators.

I then called Barnaby Tweed and told him to bring the bracelet and to hurry if he wanted the break on the story.

"Can't you tell me now?" he begged.

"Yes, but I won't," I replied and hung up. With a sigh I sought a chair. "We'll wait here a few minutes," I said. "That will give them a chance to get here."

"A good idea. Duncan sent for a doctor."

"For me?" I queried.

Peter nodded.

"Sheer nonsense. I don't want doctors fussing over me."

"You can send him away when he comes. In the meantime suppose you tell me how you knew all this."

"Can't you wait?" I snapped. "I'll have to tell Duncan; there's no point in repeating it."

When we went back to the building the men were still working on the files in the hall. Chitter greeted me warmly. "Are you all right, Miss Thomas?" At my nod he went on, "I didn't know you was one of them lady detectives; I thought you were . . ." He flushed.

"Just a meddlesome old busybody," I finished for him with a smile.

He grinned. "You're all right," he approved warmly.

Duncan's greeting was not nearly so warm. "We've been waiting for you," he said. "Come along."

"Just a moment. Has Helen Conklin arrived?"

"Yes, and that pest Barnaby Tweed. He claims to have something for you."

"He has. Did you let him in?"

Duncan nodded. "I suppose you know you came within an inch of dying," he said.

"Yes, I know."

"I'd rather have your luck than a license to steal," he growled with some return of his good nature. "Suppose you tell your story. I can fit some of the pieces together but since you did hold out on me I want to know it all."

We went into Martinique's office. Henrietta and Stella were there and were relieved to see that I was quite all right. Flannigan, Enrico, Miss Alvera, Dast still dressed as I had seen him that morning, Alice French gripping his hand as if it were her Rock of Ages. They were all there under strong police guard. Chitter, believe it or not, was casting admiring glances in the direction of Harold in his makeup.

"Miss Thomas has something interesting to tell us," Duncan said.

"I can tell you something that will interest you right now, Inspector," Miss Alvera snapped. "That is not a woman. That is Harold Dast, the man you are hunting for." She pointed an accusing finger at Harold alias Helen Conklin.

"A man!" Chitter exclaimed, aghast. His mouth dropped open, his eyes were incredulous as he peered at Harold.

"All right, Harold, you can be yourself," I said.

"What else do you have up your sleeve?" Duncan asked with an amused twinkle in his eyes.

I told him Harold's story of his observations as he stood behind the grill watching the room.

"That's it, that's it," he agreed. "You're wonderful." In his enthusiasm he gave me a good hearty whack on the back which slid my transformation into the knob on my head and made me wince with pain. But I didn't mind the pain. I knew I'd been forgiven for having deceived him.

"I'm sorry," he said contritely as he saw me manipulating the transformation.

"Think nothing of it!"

"Are you ready to go ahead?" he asked. "It's your show, yours and Dast's."

I started with my first interview with Martinique in the room. I skimmed over my reasons for being there. I didn't trust Tweed's rapidly moving pencil. I told of my return to the room and the finding of the body. Of my trip to the apartment next door and the things that happened there, of my terror, my effort to escape, of my encounter with Enrico in the hall, of the discovery of the stain on my bodice, my return to the hotel and our summons back with Chitter.

I covered the points as briefly as I could but I had to paint in the entire picture. I retold Harold's story in more detail, emphasizing all that he had seen as he stood behind the grill and watched all of us and our movements in the room. As they looked from me to Harold he nodded at several points to corroborate my statements.

"Dast made one error. He could not see the entrance to this room. When he saw Enrico closing a door he supposed it was the door to the hall, a natural mistake. He did not know then and I did not realize until later that he had seen Enrico as he finished hiding the body."

"Which means that I arrest you, Enrico, for a double murder, and an attempt on the lives of Miss Thomas and Peter Bradley," Duncan said.

Duncan's announcement was greeted with several gasps of relief. Miss Alvera seemed the least credulous of them all. Her eyes narrowed as she flashed Enrico a look of hate.

"Me!" he cried. "I had nothing to do with it. That old woman, she is the guilty one. She was trying to frame me in my apartment, she . . ." His dead pan was gone. His face became a picture of fear, guile and sudden craftiness. Then he lost control of himself completely. As he spoke his voice changed its pitch. It became a metallic twang which sent a chill down my spine. It was the same voice that had stopped me from contacting Duncan when with his blood-stained suit in my hands he had interrupted me with his threat of death.

"You told me Peter Bradley would hang for my death," I cried.

"She lies."

"It was you who killed Auriel Dodd. It was you who caught me when I tottered and would have fallen in the hall after sliding down the stairs. Your cuff was still wet with her blood. You killed Auriel Dodd and carried her body away, along with the money Alice French brought back with her."

"She lies. It is not true. She was not there, no one was there!" he cried out in desperation.

"Which convicts you, that statement. I was in the bed-closet but you didn't know that. You were the one person familiar with all of Martinique's plans. You were the one person who was always present. You were the only person who had any reason to fear me, or an investigation of your wardrobe. What your motives were I do not know."

"It is a frameup!" he cried in desperation to Duncan.

"I don't think so," Duncan replied.

"No! It is not a frameup." It was Miss Alvera, She bit out the words. "You are guilty. I see it now. Know why you did it. You planned to kill him all the time because he had had enough of this wicked business which was your idea. You wanted him out of the way, wanted his power, his money. It was you who ordered the ticket for the plane so that when he was dead I would think that he planned to go away and leave me." She turned to Duncan. "He was afraid of airplanes. I could not understand the ticket, could not believe that he would fly. Enrico made me think that I was to be left behind."

She strode across the room, her eyes darting fire. "I see it all now. It was you who sent the telegram to the French girl and signed Dast's name to it so that she would bring back the money. You wanted me, and the police, to think that Dast had killed him. You wanted me to believe that he . . ." Her words were lost in the resounding slap which cut across his face. "You killed him, I will kill you!"

He cowered before the strength of her fury, shrinking back, terror in his eyes. Her fingers clawed at him.

"No, no, no!" he cried, desperately afraid.

Her hands darted like deadly snakes. She clutched at his throat. He grabbed her wrists, trying to remove those vengeful fingers which were digging into his throat with superhuman strength.

There was something magnificent about her rage as she tried to kill him with her bare hands. She would have done it too had it not been for good old Chitter and the full strength of another man who finally pulled them apart. She stood between the two officers exuding hate, a terrifying figure, an avenging goddess, a frustrated Circe.

Enrico rubbed at his throat within the limitations of the handcuffs which had been snapped on his wrists. At a nod from Duncan, Enrico was lurched to his feet and led away.

"It's all screwy as hell to me," Tweed whispered in my ear, "but I guess I'd better print it as is. It's a wow of a story! A lot of people are going to be sitting up nights wondering about their past."

"Duncan says all that will be destroyed," I said.

"Well, I'll be running along," he said, getting up.

I gripped his coat. "Just a moment, you have something for me," I reminded him.

He handed me the bracelet carefully wrapped. "What's the dope on that? You didn't mention it."

"That's my secret."

"And you won't tell?" he said hopefully.

"Certainly not. What do you want, the earth?" I demanded with a smile at his impish face. He was like a race horse champing at the bit. "If you ever mention the bracelet to a soul, I'll . . ."

"Save your threats," he grinned. "I've seen one mad woman today and that's enough for me. I want you for a friend."

"Friendship it is, and thank you, Barnaby." I extended my hand but that thoroughly audacious young man ignored it. Instead he put his arms about me, gave me a resounding kiss on my right cheek and whispered into my ear, "I wish you were about twenty, we'd go places."

I know I beamed. "Stop your nonsense!" I snapped. "Print your story before some bright reporter steals your thunder."

"How about lunch tomorrow?" he said before he dashed for the door. "It's a date," he assured me and was gone.

Henrietta was looking in my direction with a Well-I-must-say glance. This ordeal had evidently only softened her temporarily. "Need we stay any longer?" she asked Duncan in her best Park Avenue manner.

"The case is closed for the moment. I may need some of you to give testimony at the trial. Keep in touch with me." As we prepared to leave he came over to me and said, "Some day I'd like to hear all of this story, the real dope between you and Tweed. I take it, it has nothing to do with the case or you would have told me now."

"Off the record?" I asked.

"Off the record," he repeated.

"Then come over to the hotel for dinner some evening. I owe you a hundred apologies. I appreciate your consideration. I don't think I'll ever lie to or conceal anything from the police again."

"Until the next time," he said sagely. "Americans are all alike. Unfortunately they just don't trust a policeman."

Henrietta and her brood were in the main gallery. Flannigan had waited to suggest that I get in touch with him at his office. Harold and Alice French were waiting for me.

"You did help us," she said. "I didn't mean to treat you so badly. Harold says he has explained what happened."

I nodded. She was more cuddly than ever. Her eyes had lost that haunted look. She was happy. Her hand went to her lips.

"Now," Harold cautioned, "you promised to quit that." She was like a little child caught in an overt act as she put her hands guiltily behind her.

I handed Harold the bracelet. "And now," I said, "I'll have what's left of my four thousand dollars."

He had the impudence to smile as he said, "I can't give it to you."

"You haven't . . ." I stopped because I knew from the proud look in his eyes that everything was all right. To see that look of regeneration was worth more than the money.

"It's in an envelope at the hotel waiting for you. I didn't want anything to happen to it if I found it necessary to run."

"Thank you," I said heartily. "And, thanks for trusting me today. I appreciate it. It was you who solved the case. If you ever need help, get in touch with me."

"I need help right now."

I didn't expect him to be so prompt with a request, but I had invited it.

"Will you do me a favor right now?"

"Certainly."

"Then accept these, both of them." He slipped those bracelets on my arms.

"But I can't accept them," I protested.

"Please. I can't keep them. If anything should ever come up about them you can say you bought them from Martinique. No one will doubt your word. It is the simplest, the easiest way out for me unless you think I ought to confess and take the consequences," he said so sincerely that I believed him.

"You've had music enough," I replied.

"Thank you."

"But your mother," I protested before I remembered that the gracious acceptance of a gift is just as important as the gift itself.

"She knows all about it. I talked to her on the telephone. Oh, yes, that call to New York is on your bill. I'll send you a check for it. As soon as we can, we are going to get married and go to Honolulu for a month or two and then I'm going to begin all over again."

"Good luck," I said, secretly proud of those bracelets.

As I joined the others Stella said, "Where did you get those adorable bracelets?"

"I bought them from Martinique," I replied, deciding that I might just as well begin with the deception right then and there.

THE END

Resurrected Press Books in *The Chief Inspector Pointer Mystery* <u>Series</u>

Murder at Bridge

When an afternoon bridge party attended by some of Hamilton's leading citizens ends with the hostess being murdered in her boudoir, Special Investigator Dundee of the District Attorney's office is called in. But one of the attendees is guilty? There are plenty of suspects: the victim's former lover, her current suitor, the retired judge who is being blackmailed, the victim's maid who had been horribly disfigured accidentally by the murdered woman, or any of the women who's husbands had flirted with the victim. Or was she murdered by an outsider whose motive had nothing to do with the town of Hamilton. Find the answer in... **Murder at Bridge**

One Drop of Blood

When Dr. Koenig, head of Mayfield Sanitarium is murdered, the District Attorney's Special Investigator, "Bonnie" Dundee must go undercover to find the killer. Were any of the inmates of the asylum insane enough to have committed the crime? Or, was it one of the staff, motivated by jealousy? And what was is the secret in the murdered man's past. Find the answer in... **One Drop of Blood**

AVAILABLE FROM RESURRECTED PRESS!

GEMS OF MYSTERY
LOST JEWELS FROM A MORE
ELEGANT AGE

Three wonderful tales of mystery from some of the best known writers of the period before the First World War -

A foggy London night, a Russian princess who steals jewels, a corpse; a mysterious murder, an opera singer, and stolen pearls; two young people who crash a masked ball only to find themselves caught up in a daring theft of jewels; these are the subjects of this collection of entertaining tales of love, jewels, and mystery. This collection includes:

- **In the Fog - by Richard Harding Davis's**

- **The Affair at the Hotel Semiramis - by A.E.W. Mason**

- **Hearts and Masks - Harold MacGrath**

AVAILABLE FROM RESURRECTED PRESS!

THE EDWARDIAN DETECTIVES
LITERARY SLEUTHS OF THE EDWARDIAN ERA

The exploits of the great Victorian Detectives, Poe's C. Auguste Dupin, Gaboriau's Lecoq, and most famously, Arthur Conan Doyle's Sherlock Holmes, are well known. But what of those fictional detectives that came after, those of the Edwardian Age? The period between the death of Queen Victoria and the First World War had been called the Golden Age of the detective short story, but how familiar is the modern reader with the sleuths of this era? And such an extraordinary group they were, including in their numbers an unassuming English priest, a blind man, a master of disguises, a lecturer in medical jurisprudence, a noble woman working for Scotland Yard, and a savant so brilliant he was known as "The Thinking Machine."

To introduce readers to these detectives, Resurrected Press has assembled a collection of stories featuring these and other remarkable sleuths in The Edwardian Detectives.

- The Case of Laker, Absconded by Arthur Morrison
- The Fenchurch Street Mystery by Baroness Orczy
- The Crime of the French Café by Nick Carter
- The Man with Nailed Shoes by R Austin Freeman
- The Blue Cross by G. K. Chesterton
- The Case of the Pocket Diary Found in the Snow by Augusta Groner
- The Ninescore Mystery by Baroness Orczy
- The Riddle of the Ninth Finger by Thomas W. Hanshew
- The Knight's Cross Signal Problem by Ernest Bramah

- The Problem of Cell 13 by Jacques Futrelle
- The Conundrum of the Golf Links by Percy James Brebner
- The Silkworms of Florence by Clifford Ashdown
- The Gateway of the Monster by William Hope Hodgson
- The Affair at the Semiramis Hotel by A. E. W. Mason
- The Affair of the Avalanche Bicycle & Tyre Co., LTD by Arthur Morrison

RESURRECTED PRESS CLASSIC MYSTERY CATALOGUE

Journeys into Mystery
Travel and Mystery in a More Elegant Time

The Edwardian Detectives
Literary Sleuths of the Edwardian Era

Gems of Mystery
Lost Jewels from a More Elegant Age

E. C. Bentley
Trent's Last Case: The Woman in Black

Ernest Bramah
Max Carrados Resurrected:
The Detective Stories of Max Carrados

Agatha Christie
The Secret Adversary
The Mysterious Affair at Styles

Octavus Roy Cohen
Midnight

Freeman Wills Croft
The Ponson Case
The Pit Prop Syndicate

J. S. Fletcher
The Herapath Property
The Rayner-Slade Amalgamation
The Chestermarke Instinct
The Paradise Mystery
Dead Men's Money

The Middle of Things
Ravensdene Court
Scarhaven Keep
The Orange-Yellow Diamond
The Middle Temple Murder
The Tallyrand Maxim
The Borough Treasurer
In the Mayor's Parlour
The Saftey Pin

R. Austin Freeman
*The Mystery of 31 New Inn from the Dr. Thorndyke
Series*
*John Thorndyke's Cases from the Dr. Thorndyke
Series*
The Red Thumb Mark from The Dr. Thorndyke Series
The Eye of Osiris from The Dr. Thorndyke Series
A Silent Witness from the Dr. John Thorndyke Series
The Cat's Eye from the Dr. John Thorndyke Series
*Helen Vardon's Confession: A Dr. John Thorndyke
Story*
As a Thief in the Night: A Dr. John Thorndyke Story
*Mr. Pottermack's Oversight: A Dr. John Thorndyke
Story*
*Dr. Thorndyke Intervenes: A Dr. John Thorndyke
Story*
The Singing Bone: The Adventures of Dr. Thorndyke
The Stoneware Monkey: A Dr. John Thorndyke Story
*The Great Portrait Mystery, and Other Stories: A
Collection of Dr. John Thorndyke and Other Stories*
The Penrose Mystery: A Dr. John Thorndyke Story
The Uttermost Farthing: A Savant's Vendetta

Arthur Griffiths
The Passenger From Calais
The Rome Express

Fergus Hume
The Mystery of a Hansom Cab
The Green Mummy
The Silent House
The Secret Passage

Edgar Jepson
The Loudwater Mystery

A. E. W. Mason
At the Villa Rose

A. A. Milne
The Red House Mystery
Baroness Emma Orczy
The Old Man in the Corner

Edgar Allan Poe
The Detective Stories of Edgar Allan Poe

Arthur J. Rees
The Hampstead Mystery
The Shrieking Pit
The Hand In The Dark
The Moon Rock
The Mystery of the Downs

Mary Roberts Rinehart
Sight Unseen and The Confession

Dorothy L. Sayers
Whose Body?

Sir William Magnay
The Hunt Ball Mystery

Mabel and Paul Thorne
The Sheridan Road Mystery

Raoul Whitfield
Death in a Bowl

And much more!
Visit ResurrectedPress.com
for our complete catalogue

About Resurrected Press

A division of Intrepid Ink, LLC, Resurrected Press is dedicated to bringing high quality, vintage books back into publication. See our entire catalogue and find out more at www.ResurrectedPress.com.

About Intrepid Ink, LLC

Intrepid Ink, LLC provides full publishing services to authors of fiction and non-fiction books, eBooks and websites. From editing to formatting, from publishing to marketing, Intrepid Ink gets your creative works into the hands of the people who want to read them. Find out more at www.IntrepidInk.com.

www.ingramcontent.com/pod-product-compliance
Lightning Source LLC
Chambersburg PA
CBHW071325250626
47159CB00004B/1459